Rescuing His Forever

Cameron Hart

Published by Cameron Hart, 2024.

This is a work of fiction. Similarities to real people, places, or events are entirely coincidental.

RESCUING HIS FOREVER

First edition. March 4, 2024.

Copyright © 2024 Cameron Hart.

ISBN: 979-8227881182

Written by Cameron Hart.

Want a free book?

Sign up for my newsletter[1] and get your free copy of Chasing Stacy!

One look at the stunning waitress carrying the weight of the world on her shoulders, and I'm a goner. I wasn't looking for a sweet little thing with auburn hair and more baggage than I can fit on the back of my bike, but there's no going back now. She's mine. I'll prove to her I'm more than capable of handling her past and making her feel safe again.

---

1. https://dl.bookfunnel.com/7wbqvhsx8r

Connect with me!

Check out my website, cameronhart.net[2], for sneak previews on my latest projects.

Follow me on social media:

Facebook Page - facebook.com/cameronhartauthor
Instagram - instagram.com/cameron.hart.author
TikTok - tiktok.com/@author.cameron.hart
Goodreads - goodreads.com/16081533.Cameron_Hart
Bookbub - bookbub.com/authors/cameron-hart

Chapter 1

Keaton

"First day on the new job?" my friend and fellow Navy SEAL, Warren, asks over the phone.

"Yup," I confirm as I step in front of the mirror. My short, dark hair doesn't need much maintenance, but it doesn't hurt to double-check, especially if I'm going to be making some first impressions today.

I'm still a bit surprised every time I see my reflection. I've only been on leave from the SEALs for a week, but I've got a decent beard starting. I can't decide if I'm keeping it because I don't have the energy to shave or if I actually like it.

"You know you're going to have to string more than two or three words together at a time for this bodyguard gig, right?"

I grunt while running my fingers through the short, coarse hairs at the base of my chin and jawline.

"See, that right there is an example of not communicating clearly," the wise-ass continues. "You might have to speak in full sentences. You're not back in Qatar with the SEALs where everyone understands the nuances of your grunts and growls."

"I know," I tell him with a sigh. Stepping out of the bathroom, I grab my jacket and make sure my keys and wallet are in my pocket before heading out the door. The shitty rent-by-the-week motel, while outdated and run-down, is still an upgrade from some of the places I've slept.

My mind wanders back to the deserts of the Middle East, where nights were spent in creaky cots with temps soaring over one hundred degrees. More memories of my past pop up without my permission, taking me back to my childhood when I slept in closets and under beds to hide from my father when he was in one of his moods.

"You okay?"

I'm pulled from the barrage of pathetic images zapping my brain and forced to focus back on Warren.

"Yup," I tell him, keeping my tone even. Anyone else would drop it, but not Warren. Not my best friend, who has stuck by my side since we first deployed overseas.

"Keaton," he warns.

"I'm fine," I snap, instantly regretting it.

My friend takes a deep breath, and I can tell he's winding up to give me his two cents on my current situation. "I know you don't want to hear my opinion, but as your best friend, it's my duty to tell you when you're being a stubborn ass and getting in your own way."

"Uh-huh," I grunt, making my way to the offices of Sea Change. I'm hoping a few well-placed mumbles of half-hearted agreement will pacify Warren for now. I know he means well, but I'm in no mood to be lectured. Again. Hearing all of this from my Commanding Officer the first time was hard enough.

"I'm serious. You haven't told me much about your old man, but from what I've gathered, he was a piece of shit."

This earns him a growl of agreement.

"Even so. He died. You're his only living relative. That has to mean something somewhere down deep. Whether we like it or not, our parents hold a position of power in our lives."

"Not anymore. Not from the urn his ashes are in."

Warren lets out an exasperated sigh, but hey, at least I'm stringing more than three words together, right?

"Just because you called the hospital and arranged for his body to be cremated doesn't mean you've dealt with his death."

"Seems like I did from my perspective. As the only living relative, I dealt with the remains. They're currently packed away in the storage unit with the rest of the shit I don't need or use anymore."

"You know that's not what I mean, but I'm done preaching at you. I just want you to know you're welcome to visit me again in Cali for a bit during your leave. How much time do you have off?"

"C.O. told me three months minimum. Can you fuckin' believe it? Either forced bereavement leave or early retirement. For what? *Emotional issues*? That's some bullshit, is what it is."

"And instead of taking time to reflect or holding a funeral or some kind of memorial service, you jumped into a freelance bodyguard job. No time to process, just going from one high-stakes situation to another. The grief is going to come back to you eventually, Keaton. And I don't mean that in a foreboding way. I just want you to know I'm here for you when it does."

"I don't have grief. I have annoyance that everyone seems to think they know me better than I know myself," I grumble. After a beat of silence, I clear my throat and try again. "Thanks for the sentiment, Warren. I know I have support. I just really, truly am fine with it. My father's death hasn't affected me that much, so I don't know what everyone is freaking out about."

Even as I say the words, I know they aren't true. I've always been the strong, silent type, but since my father's passing last month, I've become practically non-verbal. I have a shorter fuse than usual, and part of me knows these events are related. I'm not ready to deal with that tangled knot of raw emotion, however, so I shove it way down deep like I always do.

"Whatever you say, buddy," Warren tells me. It's his way of "agreeing to disagree," which is all I can ask for at this point.

"Thanks for checking in on me," I tell my friend truthfully. I might not be able to express myself the way other people do, but I make an effort for those who matter.

We say our goodbyes right as I approach the Sea Change offices. It's only a few blocks from my motel, making it easy to walk. The building looks a little worse for wear, but it has a professional sign and logo on the front door. For a non-profit fighting against the bigwig fishing companies on the East Coast, it's about what I pictured.

My training kicks in, and I check the perimeter for other entrances and windows, noting multiple weak spots in security. Part of my job here is to give my expert opinion on how they can keep their employees safe, and from what I'm seeing, they'll need to do some major upgrades. There are four entry points, but only one has a security camera, plus numerous windows that look like they could be shimmied open with nothing more than a butter knife. In short, this place is a nightmare.

When I finish taking notes on my phone of all the suggestions for better security, I roll my shoulders and take a cleansing breath. It's time to go inside and meet the woman I'll be in charge of for the next several weeks. Apparently, she's a force to be reckoned with when it comes to organizing protests. That's great for Sea Change but comes with risks for the fearless and perhaps a bit reckless Roxy.

I walk inside, noting that there's no buzzer for the front desk and no badge to swipe to unlock the door. In fact, the door opens right into the lobby instead of having a bit of a corridor. All negatives when it comes to security.

"Good morning," a chipper woman in her sixties says, greeting me with a warm smile. I'm not sure what to do with her kindness. It's been a long damn time since anyone has smiled at me.

"I'm Keaton, SEAL Team Alpha, reporting for the first day of bodyguard duty. I was told I would be meeting Roxy Smith here at zero-eight-hundred."

"Zero, eight... oh, you mean eight am?" the woman asks.

I nod, remembering that most civilians don't operate on military time.

"Sure thing, dear." She types away at her computer while I come to terms with the fact that this woman just called me *dear*. "Roxy will meet you in the Coral conference room, just down that hall, the first door on your left," she tells me.

I nod again and make my way in that direction, noting that I should have been escorted to my destination for security purposes, not simply sent on my way to cause unknown havoc in the office. Of course, the conference room is also unlocked, which leads me to believe every room in this building is always open.

After updating my security suggestions, I check my watch. She's ten minutes late, which might as well be an hour late in my book. The old military adage replays in my mind: *if you're not fifteen minutes early, you're late.*

I take this time to look over the file again, even though I have the thing practically memorized at this point. One can never be too prepared when taking on security detail.

Half an hour later, and I'm growing restless and frustrated. Does this woman have no respect for my time? Sure, it's not like I have anything better to do, but that's not the point. It's the principle of the matter.

I'm about to walk out to see if the disarmingly friendly woman at the front desk gave me the wrong room when the conference room door swings open. I've gone over Roxy's file a dozen times by now, which includes several pictures of her. Nothing, and I mean *nothing,* could have prepared me to meet her in real life.

She's... radiant. Her midnight black hair is pinned back to reveal her creamy skin, rounded cheeks, full lips, a button nose, and big, sparkling blue eyes. I find it hard to breathe for some reason, and my heart kicks into high gear, thudding against my chest at a rapid pace.

The woman furrows her brow at me, then opens her pouty lips before closing them again. I get it. I'm speechless, too.

But then I remember why I'm here and that she kept me waiting.

"You're late," I say, a little more harshly than I intended.

Roxy jerks back at my tone, and for the first time in a long damn time, I wish I was gentler.

Where the hell did that thought come from?

"Um, honestly, I thought my boss was joking when she said she was hiring a bodyguard for me. She said you were waiting for me here, but I didn't believe her."

"I'm no joke, and neither is your safety," I inform her, standing from my chair. Roxy is shorter than I expected and has curves for days. For some ridiculous reason, I picture how perfectly she'd fit in my arms. I could tuck her head under my chin and rock her back and forth...

What the fuck? Focus!

"I got a few freaky letters, no biggie," she says, shrugging.

"No, you received five threatening letters that have ramped up the specifics of how they'll harm you and details that lead me to believe they know more about you than you might think."

"Everyone is just being paranoid. I mean, c'mon. I'm twenty-three, a recent college grad, working at a mid-sized non-profit. I'm a little fish in the sea." Roxy pauses for a second, then snorts out the cutest little laugh. "Get it? Fish? Sea?"

She laughs at her play on words, and the sound soothes me like her joy calms me. It makes no sense, and I'm sure it's because I'm tired. Or something.

"Anyway, your services aren't needed after all," she tells me. "I'm sure we can use whatever money they are paying you on better computers or another intern or something."

"Wait a minute, now," I start, only to be cut off by the confounding woman.

"Thanks for making time to come out here, but I'll go ahead and tell my boss this whole thing is unnecessary."

"Roxy, you can't–"

"Sorry to make you come out here and waste your time on such a beautiful morning," she continues. Roxy turns her back to me and sashays out the door, disappearing behind the corner.

I'm left speechless, gaping after the whirlwind of a woman. She dismissed me? *Yeah, I don't think so, sweetheart.*

Chapter 2

Roxy

Holy hotness, Batman, I think as I step out of the conference room and turn down the nearest hallway. My heart is racing, my cheeks are flushed, and a thin sheen of sweat dots my upper lip and temples.

"Wait," the giant bodyguard calls after me. I look over my shoulder, my eyes catching on his strong arms, corded with muscle and swirling with ink.

I panic, not sure what to say or how to handle the man chasing after me. As if by some miracle, I happen to escape down the hallway where the bathrooms are located. I veer off to the right as soon as I see the women's bathroom sign, opening the door and hiding inside.

Leaning against the door, I take a second to catch my breath. *Who the hell was that?* I mean, I know who he is. He told me. He's the bodyguard my boss, Erica, hired. The thing is, I don't need a bodyguard. A few letters aren't worth all this fuss. I learned early on that words are empty. Actions are what matter.

I close my eyes against the memory of my first foster mother. When the social worker dropped me off, Mrs. Meyer invited both of us in. She made me hot chocolate with marshmallows while she and my social worker had coffee. My future foster mother said all the right things, going on about how I'd have my own room and making plans to sign me up for piano lessons and soccer. It all sounded wonderful. Too good to be true.

And it was.

As soon as the social worker pulled out of the driveway, Mrs. Meyer snatched the mug of hot chocolate out of my hands and told me to do the dishes. From then on, it was constant chores. I did end up with my own room, but it was more like a prison. Every night after dinner, I was to do the dishes and then head straight to bed so as not to annoy or aggravate Mrs. Meyer. She ensured I stayed out of the way by locking the door until she was ready to deal with me in the morning.

Taking a deep breath, I dismiss those thoughts and bring myself back into the present. I peel my back off the door and walk over to the sink, leaning over it and staring in the mirror. Just like Mrs. Meyer's words meant nothing, I'm sure whoever is behind the letters is full of shit.

I pull out my phone and log into my work email. I send my boss a quick message letting her know the bodyguard is an unnecessary expense. I even give her a few suggestions on how that money could be better spent.

I get a response immediately, which is a bit surprising. Erica is always swamped with paperwork. I thought she wouldn't even see my email until later in the day, thus giving me a few hours of peace.

Roxy—This is not up for negotiation. You're part of the Sea Change family, and you've been threatened. We take that very seriously. It's only until we can update our building security and determine who is sending the letters.

Wow. No sign-off either, which means she's in no mood to argue.

I let out a frustrated sigh and shove my phone back into my pocket before looking at myself in the mirror again. *You do not have a crush on your bodyguard,* I repeat in my head a few times. *He may be tall and muscled and sexy as sin, but he's probably an arrogant jerk who likes to throw around his weight to intimidate people.*

He certainly wouldn't be the first man I've met who used his strength for harm. Then again, even when he snapped at me, I didn't sense danger. Frustration, sure, but he never made me feel unsafe.

Probably because you were too distracted by his stubble and golden-brown eyes.

"Ugh," I say out loud, rolling my eyes at my silly thoughts.

Fine. I guess I have to handle this like the "real" adult I am. Most days, I still feel like the little lost kid who showed up on the steps of the police station at five years old with no idea where my mother had gone. I became a ward of the state shortly after and bounced around from home to home until I was finally able to graduate and go to college on a full scholarship.

Fake it 'til you make it, right? It's worked so far.

After my little pep-talk, I'm feeling a bit calmer. I open the bathroom door and run right into a freaking wall.

"Oh!" I exclaim, confused as I stumble back a bit. It takes me a second to realize I ran into my bodyguard.

His large hands wrap around my shoulders, keeping me steady. Those golden-brown eyes lock onto mine, and I can't look away. The man furrows his brow as he stares into the depths of me like he's trying to figure me out. *Good luck, buddy.*

Once I'm stable on my feet, he takes a step back. The strangest feeling washes over me like ice trickling into my veins. I'm suddenly freezing without his warm touch.

"Rule number one," the man announces, crossing his arms over his massive chest. "No running away from me."

I blink up at him a few times, wondering if he's serious about giving me rules. I've had enough ridiculous rules from foster families throughout the years to last me a lifetime.

"Rule number two," he continues in the same booming voice. "I'll need your daily schedule, including meetings and out-of-office appointments. Once I have the schedule, you'll stick to that without variation."

I stopped listening after *rule number two*. It's funny and almost cute how this giant Greek god of a man thinks he can order me around. He's so serious about everything, making me want to push his buttons and see if he ever laughs. It's hard to picture a smile on his face. I'm pretty sure his mouth is etched into a perma-scowl.

While most of me is annoyed at the list of rules he's rambling off, some long-dormant part of me is starting to wake up. I think I like the challenge. No running? *Catch me if you can.* And when he does...

An image of my bodyguard curling his fingers around the back of my neck and pulling me in for a punishing kiss flashes across my eyes. I try blinking away the fantasy before my face turns bright red.

Looking up at the man whose name I still don't know, I give him a bright smile. His eyes go wide and then narrow into slits as he stares at me suspiciously.

"I'm not much of an auditory learner," I inform him, keeping my voice light and sweet as I side-step around him. "If you could write all that out in an email for me, that would be great."

The fire in his eyes does wicked things to my body, sending a shiver down my spine. When he growls, I nearly collapse from the vibrations echoing in my chest.

"Listen here, Roxy," he starts.

"I wish I could, but I have a meeting across the hall. It's a closed meeting, but you can sit outside and work on that email."

Before he can protest again, I slip into the Sea Lily conference room, shutting the door with a click. As I shuffle my way to my favorite spot on the other side of the large table, I'm painfully aware of my erratic heartbeat and flushed cheeks. What is that man doing to me? And how long do I have to be around him?

Chapter 3

I step up to Roxy's apartment door, rolling out the tension in my neck and shoulders before lifting my hand to knock. As outlined in the stupid fuckin' email I sent her yesterday, I told her I would be at her place to pick her up at zero-seven-thirty every morning to escort her to work.

I still can't believe the sassy, five-foot, two-inch woman talked to me that way. What's even more concerning is that I let her. It's been years since I was a low enough rank to take shit from my superiors. No one talks to me the way Roxy did yesterday. She gave me orders and then dismissed me, cutting me off at every chance to defend myself.

Why is that such a turn-on?

No, goddamnit. I don't have feelings for the woman I'm in charge of protecting. She's just... she's surprising in a way I wasn't expecting. That's it. I'm always prepared, but the curvy woman with dark silky hair, blue eyes, and a feisty attitude caught me off-guard. Now I know what to expect and can plan accordingly.

After my little pep-talk, I realize Roxy hasn't so much as made a peep inside her apartment. I knock again, louder this time. The damn door rattles on its hinges, and I wince, knowing a good kick would splinter the wood, leaving Roxy vulnerable.

There's a lot about her current living situation I'm not a fan of. She's in a ground-floor apartment, for starters. The flimsy door and ancient windows make this place an easy target. I noticed the complete lack of security last night when I walked Roxy home. No cameras, only one light for the entire parking lot. And that's just what I've observed with a cursory glance. I'm sure if I dug any deeper, I'd find a thousand more things that aren't up to code.

I look at my watch, noting that she's officially late. Again.

My training kicks in, and I realize there's another reason she might not be answering her door. Jumping into action, I try the door handle, pleasantly surprised it's locked. I wouldn't put it past Roxy not to lock her door, so I'm pleased that she did this one thing for her safety.

Going over to the one window in her living room, I peer inside to catch any movement or see if I can make out any body-like lumps on the ground. My stomach drops at the thought of Roxy lying on the floor, struggling for breath.

I pry the window open, grunting as I heave the old casing up, breaking through layers and layers of paint as I go. Another safety violation.

When I have the window open enough, I haul my ass up and through the opening. I tuck my head and roll to a silent stop on my feet inside the apartment. It's empty, and from what I can see, not broken into. Everything is neat and tidy, making the small space more bearable.

My eyes land on a note on the kitchen counter next to the window I just somersaulted through. A bright pink Sticky Note lies on the counter with a loopy, feminine script scrawled upon it.

To whom it may concern, mostly my bodyguard, whose name I should know by now:

I went to work early to practice a big presentation. Make yourself at home, as I won't be needing your services.

I growl as I crumple up the piece of paper in my fist. This is the second time she's dodged me, and I must say, I don't like it. I pull out my phone and call the Sea Change office. The lady from yesterday answers the phone. I can tell because I swear I can hear her warm smile over the phone. It's as unnerving as it was the first time I met her.

"Sea Change headquarters, how may I help you?"

"This is Keaton, I'm Roxy's bodyguard. Is she there?" I hate having to ask since it makes me look incompetent, but the priority is ensuring Roxy is safe.

"Oh yes, she was here quite early. She has a special presentation she's giving to our most prestigious and generous donors. I know she's going to do great, but it's a lot of pressure for someone so young."

The woman goes on, but I stop listening. All I need is a simple yes or no.

"Thank you. I'll be right there," I say, cutting her off.

"All right, dear. See you in a bit."

I stare at my phone, then shake my head before shoving it back into my pocket. The transition to civilian life has been... strange. The small talk and pleasantries make my skin crawl, but I know it's not the receptionist's fault. I've never been particularly good at accepting kindness, let alone being called *dear*.

Fifteen minutes later, I'm walking into the office with a bone to pick with one Miss Roxy Smith. I don't bother stopping at reception, though the woman behind the desk waves to me as I turn down a hallway of conference rooms with glass doors and glass walls.

What the hell was she thinking, walking to work without me? Was my email not clear? Fuck that, I know it was flawless. I laid out our schedule, what I would need from her, what the expectations are now that she's under my care, and all the numbers, emails, etc., where she can reach me if we get separated for any reason. I just wasn't planning on the reason being my client giving me the slip at every turn.

My frustration mounts with each step, my breathing growing heavier as I think of all the ways she put herself in danger this morning. She might not care about her safety, but it's my job to protect this woman.

I pause when I hear her voice, everything in me stilling at the sound. I turn my head, catching a glimpse of Roxy in the room next to me. The door is slightly ajar, allowing me to hear her every word. She's in a navy blue wrap dress today that hugs her curves and matches her gorgeous eyes.

I notice she's wearing a bit of makeup today, unlike yesterday. It's not over the top, but it makes her eyes pop even more. Coupled with her red lipstick, Roxy looks like a goddess as she stands next to a photo of huge rolling waves on the sea projected on the wall.

"The sea is a wild, dangerous thing that cannot be tamed," Roxy starts.

Her blue eyes appear to glow the more she talks about the ocean, and I wonder for a moment if we're talking about the sea, or Roxy herself.

"The goal of Sea Change isn't to domesticate the ocean and its wildlife but to restore habitats and rehabilitate once-captured animals. We seek to keep the ocean wild and free, which means dealing with the abhorrent practices of big fishing companies worldwide. The ocean suffers the consequence, but these multi-billion-dollar companies never get reported. No one is holding them accountable. Well, now I am."

She pauses to take a breath and refocus. I can't take my eyes off of her. This woman is in her element, speaking confidently about her mission in life. I wish I were that sure of myself and what I want from my time here on earth.

"You may be wondering why I'm so obsessed with saving our oceans," Roxy continues, giving the most adorable self-effacing smile. "Truthfully, the ocean has saved me on more than one occasion. I never had a real home growing up... I... no, that's too much information," she mutters to herself. She smooths out her dress and smiles at the wall before starting again. "Growing up, when things got intense, or I felt lonely or out of place, I snuck off to whatever beach was closest."

Roxy closes her eyes and takes a deep breath. I breathe with her, wondering yet again what she's been through. I feel so connected to her at this moment, even though she has no idea I'm here. Some part of me feels like I'm intruding on a personal moment, but then I remember I'm her bodyguard. I should have been here from the very beginning.

"Sitting in the sand with the cool water lapping at my feet grounded me in a way I've never felt before," Roxy goes on. "The steady rhythm of the waves and the ocean's heartbeat calmed me on those dark nights and gave me a sense of belonging. Now, I'm older, and I have the power to make a difference. So do you."

The enchanting woman gets more into her talking points about overfishing, trawling the ocean floor, and the harm done by abandoned fishing equipment. The more she talks, the more enraptured I am by her. She's confident and brilliant, yet humble in her quest to save the sea. She's inviting people to join her, not simply throw money at the problem, but to genuinely care.

Her mesmerizing voice stops, which pulls me out of my trance. I look up, catching Roxy's eyes. Her cheeks are tinged with pink as if she's feeling a little guilty about ditching me this morning. I furrow my brow and set my jaw, but it's mostly to help me remember she's a client who disobeyed me, not a stunning woman with enough passion and eloquence to knock me on my ass.

Roxy lifts her chin in my direction, and I take that as my cue to enter. *Remember, she's a client—a client who put herself in danger.*

Even as I think the words, I know I'm fucked. I've seen a side of her I can't unsee, and every moment in her presence is going to tie me closer to her. I can feel it already.

Chapter 4

Roxy

Yup. He's as tall and muscled and devilishly handsome as he was yesterday. I hoped he would somehow turn into a toad overnight, and I would wake up this morning not under his spell.

But here he is, all six and a half feet of him, rippling with muscles and tattoos. Those golden-brown eyes latch onto mine as he takes a step forward. My heart stutters in my chest, then kicks into high gear as the giant of a man lumbers toward me.

His shoulders take up the entire door frame, which should scare me. I've known plenty of men who would use their weight and strength to intimidate, but I'm not scared of this man. Maybe it's because I know he's hired to protect me, but I sense it's something deeper. His presence alone is calming in a way I've only ever felt when I'm near the ocean.

My bodyguard steps into my personal space, and I have to crane my head back to meet his gaze. The fire glowing in his eyes sends tendrils of sharp pleasure down my spine, and I hold my breath, not sure how to behave now that he's so close.

The man slowly lifts his hand, brushing his fingertips across my temple and down my cheek, tracing my jawline until he reaches my neck. His warm, calloused hands make every part of my skin prickle with awareness at his touch. What would it feel like to have his fingertips grazing up my thigh, over my breasts, down, down, down...

"My name is Keaton," he says gruffly as he cups the back of my neck.

I let out my breath, trembling slightly from his touch. His hold isn't rough or angry; it's more like he's letting me know this is important, and he wants my full attention.

"Keaton," I repeat, nodding in acknowledgment.

"What happened this morning cannot happen again," he says, never breaking eye contact. "You broke rules one through four, and it's barely eight in the morning."

"Give me time, and I'm sure I can break a few more by lunch," I blurt, mostly out of nervousness. My voice is a little louder than I meant it to be, but I'm having a hard time controlling anything, let alone the volume of my voice.

Keaton frowns at me, but I swear I saw a glint of amusement in his golden gaze. I'll take it. He drops his hand from the back of my neck and takes a step back as if I suddenly burned him. Like yesterday, I'm freezing now that he's not touching me.

"I don't appreciate the sarcasm, and I won't allow you to pull another stunt like you did at your apartment earlier."

Oh, hell no. He won't allow *me?*

I feel the anger rising from deep inside me as I remember all the times I was controlled growing up. However, I can't open that can of worms right now, so I plaster on my brightest smile. I love how it confuses Keaton.

"It's my job to keep you on your toes," I reply.

The man blinks at me a few times, then frowns. I didn't think his eyebrows could get any angrier, but they're so bunched together now that they look like one big unibrow. Still sexy, though. Dammit.

"That's the opposite of your job," he growls.

That sound should scare me, but I find myself responding to it in the most inappropriate way. I squeeze my thighs together, hoping to find some relief from the dull, throbbing ache in my core.

"Your job is to follow my orders so I can keep you safe," he states. "End of story."

He crosses his arms over his broad chest and stares down at me. I put my hands on my hips and square off with this equally bossy and sexy man.

"I don't respond well to people ordering me around," I inform him, putting on my best scowl. "I've had enough of men telling me how to behave, women telling me how to fit in, foster parents yelling about me not doing enough or being enough, and... I just... I'm..." I trail off, trying to catch my breath. I didn't realize how worked up I was, or apparently, how triggering it would be to be "ordered" to do something.

Keaton stands silently beside me, not saying anything, while I take a few calming breaths. He doesn't push or pry; he simply exists next to me as a solid, unwavering presence until I feel somewhat in control of my body again.

"You need someone to protect you the same way you're protecting the ocean," Keaton says after a beat of silence. I turn my head in his direction, our eyes meeting. He looks a little softer now, less prickly and sharp. "I'm not trying to control you, Roxy. I understand that you're wild and untamed, like the sea you love so much."

I can't look away from Keaton. No one has ever listened and understood me with so few words.

"My goal is to keep you safe," he continues. "I can't do that if I don't know where you are. Do you understand?"

I nod. "I'm not used to people caring about where I am or why," I admit for some reason.

"I know," is all he says. It's enough.

"So, um, have you–"

We're interrupted by a knock on the open conference room door. I jerk my head in that direction, smiling at Cindy, our receptionist.

"The donors are ready for you in the Sand Dollar conference room," she tells me, a small smile curling up the corner of her lips. She darts her eyes between Keaton and me with a knowing look.

"Thanks, Cindy," I tell her, not wanting her to assess me any further. I have no idea why I'm reacting to Keaton this way, but I don't want to share my feelings with Cindy, however sweet she may be.

She nods and steps out into the hallway to return to her desk. I turn my back to Keaton, not sure what to say. As I gather everything I'll need for my presentation, I mentally rehearse the first few lines.

"Roxy," comes Keaton's deep, rich voice. I freeze in place, turning slowly to face my bodyguard. I have to brace myself for the impact of his stare. He's a force of nature, much like the ocean itself. Maybe that's why I'm so drawn to him. "If you're half as passionate and well-spoken in your presentation as you were in your practice run, you're going to knock 'em dead."

I'm shocked by his compliment, my mouth opening and closing like a confused fish until I nod and tuck a few strands of hair behind my ear. I have no response, so I shuffle around him and step across the hall to the correct room.

Before closing the door, I look over my shoulder at Keaton, standing with his arms crossed and his eyes trained on me. I should feel exposed or uncomfortable, but truthfully, I like having his attention. I like it way too much.

Which is a problem.

I can't get used to someone having my back, someone to listen to me and understand where I'm coming from. Plus, this is just a job for him. It's not like the sexiest, growliest man alive would look twice at an overweight marine biologist nerd who barely makes ends meet with the paycheck from the non-profit she works at. I'm not exactly a catch.

Clearing my throat, I shove all thoughts of Keaton aside and get everything set up for my presentation. When I'm in the zone, nothing can get to me. Right now, I'm cruising through my presentation, hitting on all the most devastating effects of deep-sea fishing while weaving in my personal connection to the ocean.

By the end of it, I'm surrounded by mostly men and a few women dressed in various shades of black and gray power suits. I know a few of them are skeptical, but the vast majority of people sitting around the conference table are smiling and nodding along. One woman takes out a tissue and dabs at her eyes. I didn't think my presentation was *that* good, but I hope the emotional response translates to more donations.

My boss and the director of Sea Change steps up to the front of the room, thanking me and shaking my hand. I nod and give her a smile, hoping I did a good job. When she gives me a subtle thumbs up, I know we must have a few big checks coming our way.

She talks for a few more minutes about the budget and more of the nitty-gritty business side of things while I let my mind wander. It's always such a rush to share my story and to know I'm making waves. I smile at my joke, even though I know it makes me a total dork.

We're all dismissed, and in the rush of people exiting the conference room, I somehow lose sight of Keaton. He was right outside the room the entire time. I didn't dare look over at him, but I felt his steady, soothing presence nonetheless.

A wicked thought occurs, and even though I know it's a bad idea, I can't resist. My short stature is to my advantage as I hide amongst the throng of suits leaving the Sea Change building.

Once outside, I look around, half-expecting Keaton to jump out and drag me back. When he doesn't appear, I decide to treat myself to a latte and a scone from the cute little cafe across the street.

As soon as I walk into the cafe, an unsettling sensation washes over me. I feel eyes on me, but not like when Keaton is watching me. I'm probably just being paranoid. As much as I hate to admit it, the threatening letters have gotten to me. Still, I have to stay strong. I can't let anyone know I have a weakness or can be taken down with a few words on a piece of paper.

I straighten my back and hold my chin high as I step up to the counter and order my drink and scone. After waiting at the end of the counter for my latte and food, I make my way to a table against the back wall. Even though I'm tucked away in the corner, I still feel vulnerable, like anyone could come sit down next to me.

It's silly for me to be this upset, this scared, especially when I dodged my bodyguard - again - to get this little slice of peace and quiet. Only, I'm not at peace. I'm on high alert, the hairs on the back of my neck prickling with anxiety.

I lift my latte to my lips, frowning when I spill a bit on the table. I didn't realize my hands were shaking that badly.

The door to the cafe swings open, and the all-too-familiar silhouette of my giant bodyguard fills the entryway. His eyes narrow as he scans the tables and booths until he finally sees me. That glow in his eyes intensifies, and I know I should run. Or should I stay? Let Keaton watch out for me, if only for a little bit.

No, he'll be gone soon enough, and I'll be on my own, like always.

Keaton stomps toward me, his footsteps echoing on the hardwood floor. I panic, my heart wanting to stay here while my head is screaming at me to run like hell. I have a split second to decide what to do, and the flight part of my brain takes over, propelling me from my seat and launching me headlong into the back dish room of the cafe. It's the only exit Keaton isn't blocking.

I get a few strange looks from the staff members, but mostly, everyone looks bored and unamused. Fine by me. I see the side exit on the far right of the dish room, and I sprint in that direction, the adrenaline pulsing through my veins and nearly sending me into a panic attack.

I burst through the door, tripping over my feet as I stumble outside. I can't stop. Can't slow down. I pump my arms and legs, running at a dead sprint for the first time since middle school gym class. It's as awful as I remember.

I find myself running toward my apartment as if on autopilot.

"Roxy!" Keaton calls out. Damn, that man is fast. "Roxy, stop!"

Tears sting my eyes, but I blink them away, focusing solely on making it to my apartment where I can shut the door and keep Keaton and my feelings for him out.

The shitty apartment complex I've called home for the last year comes into view, and I breathe a sigh of relief. Until I get closer and see my door hanging off of its hinges. I come to an abrupt stop, ice flooding my veins, followed by a crippling sense of being violated.

The more I see, the harder it is to breathe. My living room window is shattered, and I can see that everything has been overturned, emptied, and trampled on. Clothes are strewn about, along with pieces of broken plates and cups.

I'm stuck, unable to move, breathe, or blink.

"Are you okay?" Keaton says from behind me, resting a hand on my shoulder. I jerk away from him on instinct, and he holds his hands up in front of him in a sign of surrender. "It's me. I'm here," he says, his voice more soothing than I've ever heard it before.

Keaton holds out his hand, and I take it in mine, needing his comfort right now. He pulls me closer, then tucks me behind him, keeping one hand on my hip.

"Stay close, but stay behind me, okay?"

I nod, relieved to have someone else here who knows what to do. As independent as I like to think I am, I still feel like an aimless child some days.

Keaton searches the perimeter and then steps inside with his gun drawn. I'm fisting the back of his shirt, not wanting us to be separated.

Keaton relaxes when he's satisfied that no one is inside. Until he sees the letter on my kitchen table. The envelope is just like all the others—"Roxy" is spelled out using individual letters cut from magazines and glued in place. If I had any doubts about who was behind this break-in, they're gone now.

Keaton guides me to my bed, which has a clear spot on it. He motions for me to sit, kneeling in front of me, peering up into my eyes. "Do you believe me now?" he asks softly. "Your safety is at risk. I'm not sure how else to get through to you."

"I believe you," I whisper, my voice cracking. "I-I'm sorry."

Keaton places his hands on my thighs, drawing my attention to the movement. He starts to pull away, but I put my hands on top of his. Our eyes meet, and I see a different side of my growly bodyguard. He's worried. About me?

"I've never had anyone care about me like this before," I admit. "I don't know how to handle... all of... this." I gesture vaguely up and down his body, which earns me the tiniest smirk. God, that's dangerous. I can't imagine what his actual smile would do to me.

"Right now, all I need you to do is grab a bag and get some clothes and whatever you'll need for a few days. You'll stay with me until we figure out who is behind this."

I open my mouth to protest, but Keaton gives me a look that has the words dying on my lips.

"Let me protect you," Keaton says as he slips his hands from beneath mine. He stands, holding out his hand once again for me. I take it, surprised when he tugs me into his arms, wrapping me up in a hug. I melt into his embrace, and he squeezes me, holding all my broken pieces and confusing thoughts together. "I've got you," he murmurs, pressing a kiss to the top of my head.

Oh, lord, I'm falling for my big, burly, and unexpectedly sweet bodyguard. I just hope this doesn't end in heartbreak.

Chapter 5

Keaton

Mine.

The word settles deep in my chest and expands outward, filling every empty space in my heart. Roxy is curled into my embrace as I hold her close with one hand on her lower back. My other hand gently strokes her silky black hair, hoping to soothe her fears.

"Let's get you packed up," I say softly, my lips brushing the shell of her ear. "The sooner we get out of here, the better."

Roxy nods and slowly untangles herself from me. I don't like it. I can't fathom how I've lived on this planet for thirty-seven years without the curvy little goddess by my side.

I watch the woman I'm falling for wander around her small living space, picking up a few things here and there and then placing them down somewhere else. She looks so fragile at this moment, so lost and vulnerable. Her face is pale, and she's barely holding back tears. I hate seeing her like this. Where did the confident, brilliant, charismatic woman from this morning's presentation go? I vow to bring her back and vanquish her fears for good.

"Here," I say, trying to keep my tone even so as not to startle her.

I hand her an empty backpack I found lying on top of a pile of clothes. Roxy takes the backpack and blankly stares at it. My poor girl is about to crash from the adrenaline rush. It's all too much for her, but she doesn't know how to ask for help.

I walk over to the dresser in the corner of her studio apartment, which has been turned over on its side. Shuffling through the pieces of clothing, I pick out a few outfits that will have to tide Roxy over until we can go shopping.

Making my way back over to my girl, my heart breaks when I see she's stuck in the same position, holding the backpack and staring into space. I slowly approach Roxy, wrapping my hand around hers and helping her hold the backpack open while I place the clothes inside.

"Th-thanks," she murmurs on a shaky breath.

"Why don't you grab some toiletries from the bathroom while I call the police?"

"Police?" This seems to startle Roxy out of her trance. "That's not necessary."

"Your home was broken into," I tell her sternly. "And we know who was behind it. That letter needs to go to forensics so they can run tests and figure out who sent it. Don't you want that?"

Roxy pauses and then eventually nods, though she looks defeated and exhausted. Her phone rings, startling both of us. "Crap," she says under her breath. "It's work. I've been gone for almost an hour now."

"I'll call the office and let them know you'll be taking the rest of the day off. I'm sure everyone will understand after what happened here."

At first, I think she's going to protest, but Roxy surprises me by slowly nodding in agreement. "Yeah. I think I could use some rest."

She's fading fast, and I need to get her out of here and tucked into a warm bed.

Ten minutes later, I've made all the necessary calls and arrangements, and Roxy is by my side again. I half carry, half walk her down the street a few blocks to my motel. The closer we get, the more nervous I become.

I should have rented an apartment with a temporary lease or picked a motel with less rust on the sign and decor that has been updated since the seventies. It didn't matter when it was just me. I've learned to sleep anywhere and don't need many creature comforts.

Roxy, on the other hand, deserves room service and silk sheets.

I fumble with the keys to my room, my hands growing sweaty and clammy. I can't remember the last time I was this anxious.

After getting the door open, I step inside, aware that Roxy is right behind me. She hasn't been more than two inches from me since we left her apartment, and I can feel the fear radiating off of her. While I'm glad she's taking the threats more seriously, I never wanted this to happen.

"How are you holding up?" I ask, turning to face Roxy.

"I'm good," she lies, giving me a weak smile.

"You don't have to hide from me, Roxy," I say softly, reaching for her trembling hand. I squeeze it, wanting her to hear what I'm saying. "I want the truth from now on. That's how we build trust."

After a beat of silence, Roxy finally lets out a long, exasperated sigh as she folds in on herself. "I can't show weakness," she whispers. I'm not sure I heard her correctly. "If I let them get to me, they've won."

"No one is invincible," I say, though I'm unsure if I'm talking to Roxy or myself. I can relate to not wanting to let the bad guys win. Some part of me feels like if I face my dad's death and forgive him for the vile things he did during his life, I'm letting him win.

Roxy shivers and gasps as the first tear falls. I'm right here, pulling her into my arms and cradling her while she cries out all of her anxiety, fear, and exhaustion.

When she's done, I lean back just enough to rest my forehead on hers. Our noses are almost touching, and her warm breath skates across my lips with each exhale. "You're safe here, Roxy," I murmur. "You're safe with me."

"I know," she whispers back. "Thank you."

I almost don't hear her last two words, but my already heavy heart sinks when they register. It kills me that she's thanking me. It speaks volumes about what she's been through that her safety is a luxury.

"There are fresh towels in the bathroom. Would a warm shower feel good?" I ask, noting how my girl is still shivering.

Roxy nods, which seems to be about all she's capable of at the moment. I lead her to the small bathroom and turn the water on to heat before grabbing her backpack and setting it on the sink counter.

"I'll be right out here making a few calls."

She nods but doesn't make eye contact.

"Hey," I say softly as I reach out and tip her chin up with a crooked finger. Those blue eyes are rimmed in red, and her bottom lip trembles slightly as she meets my gaze. "You're safe," I tell her again. "I'm not going to let anything happen to you."

With that, I turn and leave the bathroom before I do something totally inappropriate, like kiss her pouty lips and claim her as mine.

Once I'm back in the main room, I pull out my phone and search for Watchdog Protection, Inc. A former military buddy of mine started up his own security firm with several of his friends. They handle everything from consultations for security upgrades to bodyguard-for-hire services. He was the one who suggested this job to me.

"Keaton, I was hoping to hear from you soon," Logan says after I find the correct number and call him. "How's the job? Not too boring, I hope."

"Not at all," I say with a slight smirk, thinking back to how Roxy told me her job was to keep me on my toes.

"Uh-oh. Is that good or bad?" Logan's tone changes, and I know he's in mission mode now.

"Both, but right now, I need your help with the bad part."

"Both?" he questions.

"Let's just say you're not the only one who fell for a client."

Logan chuckles over the phone, no doubt reminiscing about his now-wife, Spencer. The two met while he was on the job, and they've been blissfully married and living out their happily ever after for the last few years.

"Good for you, K. Seriously. Spencer makes me better in every way, and I hope your girl does the same for you."

"She's amazing," I admit. I can feel the tips of my ears turning red and my cheeks flushing slightly. I've never talked this way about a woman before, and I'm afraid it's going to be cheesy as hell. Then again, Logan understands. "But she has some relentless enemies who just escalated the threats. They broke into her house this morning and left another letter."

I didn't tell Roxy I read the letter while she was packing her personal things in her bathroom. I was careful not to touch the envelope or letter with my bare hands so I wouldn't leave fingerprints. I wanted the police to have the letter, but I needed to know what it said.

"Shit," Logan mutters, bringing me back to the present.

"Yeah. It was the worst yet. It detailed that they had been watching her. It's only a matter of time before they silence her for good." My stomach churns as I think about the explicit way they wrote about harming Roxy, and how no one would know.

"Whatever you need from us, we've got your back," my friend assures me.

"The physical letter is with law enforcement, but I have pictures. I figured between the cops and us working on this, we should be able to find out who is doing this once and for all."

"Send over the photos and any other information you have. I'll have our tech guy search the evidence for clues and report back."

I thank him, and we hang up just as Roxy steps out of the bathroom. Steam curls behind her, and I'm momentarily struck dumb at the sight of my girl in leggings and a tank top, her long, damp hair hanging over one shoulder like a black, inky river.

Roxy stands awkwardly in the doorway, folding her arms around her stomach as if hugging herself. I pat the seat next to me on the small couch, and my girl pads her cute little feet over to where I am. She looks at the tiny space on the couch and then at me. I realize I'm taking up far more than half of the loveseat with my bulky arms and legs, so I pat my knee and wait to see what she does.

"Oh. You want me to... sit... on your lap?" she asks slowly, as if not believing me.

I nod and pat my knee again.

"I'm far too heavy for–"

I can't even let her finish that sentence. I reach out and loop my arm around her waist, pulling the curvy goddess closer until she's standing between my spread legs. "You're perfect," I tell her, making sure she hears me when I say it. "If you're comfortable enough with me, then I would very much like to have you right here in my arms, on my lap."

"For bodyguard reasons?" Roxy asks, a slight smile curling up one corner of her mouth.

"Amongst other things," I say, giving her a wink.

Roxy's eyebrows shoot up to her forehead, and I won't lie; I like surprising her like this. For once, I'm the one keeping her on her toes.

The beautiful, brave woman who has been through so much in her life gives me a smile that's somehow equal parts sweet, vulnerable, and sassy. It's everything Roxy is and everything I didn't know I needed.

I guide my girl to sit on my lap, which she does. Her back is straight and tense, so I run my fingertips up and down her spine, hoping to relax her. When she curls up and rests her head on my shoulder, I finally feel complete. I adjust her slightly so her legs are stretched out across mine, and then I hold her, rocking her gently back and forth until I hear her soft, even breaths.

Roxy is sound asleep in my arms. I want to pound my fist on my chest in pride that I could make her comfortable and safe enough to sleep after everything that happened this morning.

As I look down at the sleeping princess, I wonder, not for the first time, how I survived this long without her in my life. I need to find out who is after my girl, and then I need to make her mine. Forever.

Chapter 6

Roxy

I slowly blink my heavy eyelids a few times, adjusting to the light in the room. As my vision clears, I realize I have no idea where I am. The window is small and partially covered with olive green and mustard yellow curtains.

The more I wake up, the more I notice. Wood paneling? Did I fall into a time machine? But no, I'm in a bed with slightly scratchy blankets. *When did I go to bed?* The last thing I remember is...

I'm suddenly aware of someone else in the bed with me. I'm on my side with my back facing the other side of the bed, and I don't dare look over my shoulder to see who it is. My heart jackhammers against my ribcage, and panic weaves its way around my chest, squeezing until I can hardly breathe.

"It's just me," a familiar voice says.

Keaton.

Everything in me relaxes as I let out a relieved sigh and turn to face him. He's close. Much closer than I thought he'd be. We're nose to nose, only a few inches apart.

"Hi," I whisper, like an idiot.

Keaton grins, and holy crap, I was right. It's sexy and playful and perfect.

"Hi."

We just stare at each other for who knows how long. I take in his angular jaw, dotted with stubble, his strong nose, and surprisingly full lips. I watch in fascination as his golden-brown eyes dart around my face like he can't get enough of me.

"You're so beautiful, Roxy," he murmurs, his breath fluttering across my lips.

Keaton ghosts his fingertips along my eyebrow, temple, and cheek, then down my neck. I swear I feel that small touch *everywhere*. I throb in places I've never throbbed before.

I lean into his touch, moving ever so slightly closer to him. Keaton moves closer, too, until our noses are touching. My heart beats out of my chest, and every nerve ending is alive and sensitive.

Without thinking, I place a palm on Keaton's chest, which makes him groan softly. I can feel him trembling slightly underneath my touch. Am *I* doing that to him?

Encouraged by his response, I tilt my head and press my lips to his in my first kiss ever.

When he doesn't respond right away, I pull back, absolutely mortified that I misread the situation. But then Keaton curls his fingers into my messy hair and holds me in place while his lips crash down on mine.

It's possessive and passionate and perfect. His mouth is firm, soft, and commanding. And then he licks the seam of my lips. I moan for him, the sensation sending an unexpected shot straight to my clit.

Keaton slips his tongue inside of my mouth and kisses me in long, steady strokes. My hand slides up from his chest to the back of his neck as I pull him closer so I can taste more. I tangle my tongue with his, showing him I want this as much as he does.

He groans and then nips my bottom lip, making me gasp. Keaton grins wickedly and then dives back in, exploring my mouth and eating me right up. I have to tear myself away from him to get some air. Keaton growls when I break contact with him, but he doesn't let me get very far.

I feel him press soft kisses down my jaw and then nip at my pulse point. I gasp and moan when my pussy clenches at the sensation. Keaton must sense it, too, because he does it again and again, nipping the sensitive spot and then sucking on it.

"You're incredible," he whispers before kissing me again, slower this time.

He's showing me that he'll take care of all of me with this kiss. He's passionate and possessive while also treating me like I'm somehow precious.

When we pull apart, Keaton rests his forehead on mine, his labored breathing matching mine.

"Thank you," I say like a total dork. "I mean because, like.... I mean, I've never..." I stutter, rolling away from him as my face burns bright red with embarrassment.

He doesn't let me get very far. "Come back here." He places his large hand on my hip and rolls me back into his solid chest. "New rule. You're not allowed to be embarrassed in front of me. Ever."

I crack a smile at his serious demeanor and the way he thinks he can command my embarrassment to leave.

"I'm not sure that's how it works," I point out, raising an eyebrow at him.

"I know. I should know by now not to give you rules," he grumbles, though his eyes have a spark of playfulness. I like this side of Keaton. I like all sides of my giant, sexy-as-hell bodyguard, but I'm happy to see him smiling more.

"That's not what I meant," I sigh, lightly swatting at his chest. Keaton takes my hand, turning it over so he can kiss the inside of my wrist. I can feel his lips everywhere, and I know he knows it when he smirks at me.

"Were you trying to tell me you've never kissed anyone, beautiful?"

I blink a few times at his pet name for me. Beautiful? Me? Seriously? Compared to him?

"Roxy?" Keaton asks, a hint of worry in his voice.

"Yes," I finally admit. "I just... I don't know. Growing up, I had too much drama going on at whatever foster home I was in at the time to worry about boys or dating."

Keaton combs his fingers through my hair and then strokes the bare skin of my arm, encouraging me to continue.

"And then when I aged out of the system and got my scholarship, I hit the books and spent most weekends in the library to make sure I kept my grades up for my scholarship."

"There's no reason to be ashamed of that," he says softly. "I didn't date much in high school for similar reasons, only it was my old man, not foster families."

I rest my hand over his heart, wanting to know everything about this man's story.

"And when I finally escaped that hellhole, I joined the military and shipped off to basic as soon as I could. Haven't looked back since. Between working my way up the ranks and deployments over the years, I haven't had much time for women, let alone a relationship."

Keaton places his hand over mine on his heart, closing his eyes and taking a deep breath. When he opens them again, his golden gaze is filled with vulnerability. "I guess what I'm saying is that this is new for me, too. We'll learn together, yeah?"

I smile and nod, leaning in for another kiss. Keaton gladly opens up for me as I take control this time, exploring his mouth and drawing out sounds of pleasure.

Suddenly, Keaton pulls away, nearly making me topple forward into him. I catch myself at the last minute, then furrow my brow at the confusing man.

"We're going on a date," he announces.

A giggle escapes my lips, and I try covering my mouth to keep in the sound. Keaton hears it and raises a brow. "Usually, a person is *asked* if they would like to go on a date," I point out.

"But then that leaves you room to say no," he answers matter-of-factly.

I laugh, letting the sensation take me over as I roll onto my back and giggle some more. It feels good to laugh after the last few days.

Keaton rolls on top of me, holding himself up with a hand on either side of my head. "Go on a date with me," he demands.

"That's not much better," I tease, unable to hold my smile back.

"What if I make it a rule that you *can't* date me? You seem awfully determined to break all of my rules." Keaton's eyes are blazing with lust, but there's a playful smirk on his lips.

"Oh. Well, that changes everything," I sass.

Keaton growls and then nuzzles into the side of my neck, his short beard tickling my skin. I laugh and shove him off of me, only to have my man switch our positions, with me sprawled out across his chest.

"Good. I'm glad we could come to an agreement."

I smack his chest and then kiss his cheek. Keaton cups the back of my neck and pulls me in for a real kiss, leaving me breathless. I don't know how this will end, but I want whatever he's offering me right now.

After a breakfast of cold bagels and coffee, Keaton heads to the shower, giving me a bit of space to call the office and ask if I can work from home, or in this case, motel, for a few days until this all blows over. My boss is in complete agreement and even offers for me to take some paid time off. I need something to occupy my mind, however, so we agree that I'll work half days until we figure out who is after me.

I open my laptop and get lost in a research project. I'm not sure how long it's been, but when a shadow passes over me, I look up to see Keaton smiling down at me.

"Hi," I squeak out, my cheeks flushing slightly. I don't know if I'll ever get used to how big and all-consuming his presence is. When Keaton looks at me, I feel like the only person in the whole world.

"Hi, beautiful," he says, leaning down to kiss the top of my head. "Is this a good time to take a break? You've been working all morning. I should feed you."

"Have I?" Sure enough, when I look at the clock on the corner of my computer screen, I see nearly four hours have passed. "Sorry. I guess I was in the zone. That must have been boring for you." I close my computer and set it aside, letting Keaton help me off the couch.

"Boring is a nice change of pace after losing you twice in one day," he teases, that playful smirk on his lips. "Besides, I wasn't bored. I was planning our date."

He nods to the tiny kitchenette in the corner of the motel room. I'm shocked to see a picnic basket and the remnants of what looks like an amazing meal he assembled and packed away.

"Wh... How...?"

"I had groceries delivered along with the biggest basket I could find. Did you know it's surprisingly difficult to find a picnic basket? Especially one that can be delivered within the hour."

I'm surprised by his thoughtfulness and that I didn't notice all this happening in the background. When I get caught up in a project, I guess the rest of the world fades away.

"So," Keaton continues after I haven't said anything. He shifts his weight from foot to foot, then rubs the back of his neck, almost like he's nervous. "Ah, it might be kind of lame, but I was thinking we could have a picnic on the beach. I know you love the ocean, and I wanted to take you somewhere you felt at peace. Plus, being out in a crowded restaurant in public... it's just better to be somewhere more secluded."

He looks away from me, and I realize he's anxious about his plans, which is crazy. I reach out for his hand, weaving my fingers with his. Keaton looks at me, clearly wanting some kind of approval. "This is the most thoughtful thing anyone has ever done for me," I say softly. "I can't believe you went through all this trouble."

My surprisingly sweet bodyguard lifts my hand to his mouth, pressing a kiss to my knuckles before pulling me into his arms. "You're worth so much more than this. I want to spoil you. I will. As soon as it's safe and the threats have stopped, I'll take you out dancing."

"You dance?" I ask, unable to imagine the serious, stoic Keaton busting a move.

"No," he admits. "But for you, I'd make a fool of myself trying."

I smile at him, then lift on my tiptoes to kiss his cheek. Keaton holds me in place by wrapping an arm around my waist, then dives in for a real kiss. It quickly turns heated, and I grind against his thigh, trying to get enough friction to find release.

"Goddamn," he pants when we finally break apart. "We better head out before I lose my mind completely."

It's hard to believe that I hold the same power over him that he does over me. For some reason I don't understand, Keaton finds me sexy and irresistible.

"Lead the way," I tell him, stepping back and giving him room to adjust his thick erection. I can't help but stare at it. Holy crap, it's *huge*.

Keaton clears his throat and rolls out his shoulders. It gives me such wicked satisfaction to know I did that to him.

After grabbing the picnic basket, we head out into the parking lot. Keaton directs me to his truck, which looks like it was rented. He's clearly not from here if he's renting a vehicle and a motel room. The nagging doubt in the back of my mind rears its head, and I wonder where he's going after he's done with me.

I never want him to be done with me.

"Roxy?" Keaton asks.

I shake my head free of those thoughts and smile at him. He's holding the passenger side door open, and I climb in, rolling my eyes when he buckles my seatbelt.

"I'm capable of doing that on my own," I inform him.

"Bodyguard duty," he says with a wink. A freakin' wink. And I thought he couldn't get any sexier.

Keaton hops in the driver's seat, and we take off. He winds his way through back roads, taking us somewhere I've never been. I thought I knew every spot in town to catch a glimpse of the ocean, but my man is full of surprises.

He pulls into a shaded spot under a tree, then hurries to my side to open my door. He's so adorable. My heart melts knowing he's trying so hard to impress me and do everything properly. No one has ever cared for me like this.

Keaton leads me down a small hill, helping me step over a fallen branch and navigate the rocky, mostly hidden path. I'm starting to question if he knows what the ocean is and if maybe he confused it for a forest, but then we emerge out of the woods and into a clearing.

I gasp at the pristine slice of paradise. It's a small beach with soft sand and a breathtaking view of the sea. A large boulder sits off to the left, blocking this section from the bigger portion of the beach. The forest wraps around to the right, creating a perfect private hideaway.

"How did you find this?" I ask as I slip my shoes off and take a few steps onto the beach, loving the warm sand between my toes. Closing my eyes, I tilt my head up and breathe in the salty air, letting the steady rhythm of the waves lapping at the shore fill me up.

After a few moments of silence, I open my eyes and peer over my shoulder at Keaton. He's staring at me, though I can't quite read the look in his eyes. It's almost as if he's... in awe? Of me?

"You're so beautiful," Keaton whispers, coming up behind me.

He wraps his arms around my waist and pulls me toward him so my back is pressed against his chest. I let out a shuddering breath when his lips graze the shell of my ear.

"I can't believe you're here with me," he says softly.

I lean into his touch, my breath hitching when he kisses my neck. One minute, I'm surrounded by Keaton's warmth and sweet words, and the next, he's gone. I turn around to pout, but then I see him hauling the picnic basket and blanket from where he set them down.

I smile as I watch him spread the blanket several feet from the shoreline. It's close enough to enjoy this incredible oasis but far enough away that we don't get wet. He pulls out a bottle of wine and the paper cups from the motel room, making me giggle.

I join him on the blanket, my mouth dropping as I see everything he prepared. Delicious-looking croissant sandwiches, cheese and crackers, grapes, strawberries, and a jar of green olives. I give him a questioning look when he pulls the olives out, and Keaton shrugs, the tips of his ears turning red. His blush is the cutest thing I've ever seen, which seems like an oxymoron for such a muscled, growly giant.

"I looked up what foods to pack for a picnic. This came up, so I added it to the cart. Have you ever had them?"

I shake my head no. "I didn't get a lot of variety in meals growing up." Keaton frowns, and I hate that I ruined the mood. "But I'm always up for trying something new!" I say, pasting on a smile.

Keaton sets the jar down and places his hand over mine where it's resting on the blanket. "You don't have to hide from me or pretend everything is okay." His intensity is almost too much to bear, and I look away, fighting back tears for some stupid reason. "Look at me, Roxy," he says softly. When I do, his golden-brown eyes search mine, reaching down into the very depths of my soul. "I want your story. All of it. Even the painful parts. Let me in, beautiful. I promise I won't let you down."

My bottom lip trembles as I swallow past the lump in my throat. "I never met my dad, and I don't remember much about my mom, just that she was an addict with undiagnosed mental health issues. My first memory is watching her leave with her friends. I was five. She never came back."

"Roxy," Keaton murmurs, moving closer to me. I lean into him, taking solace in his embrace. He wraps an arm around my shoulders, his fingertips brushing along the bare skin of my arm in a comforting gesture.

"I don't remember how long I was alone, but I was later told it was almost three days. I just knew I was hungry and thirsty and needed help. When I figured out how to open the door, I wandered down the street and all over until I recognized a cop car. It was parked with a bunch of other cop cars, so I figured that's where the police lived and they could help."

"Did they?"

"Yeah," I whisper, nodding my head. "I wandered into the police station looking disgusting and pathetic, and social services were called right away. It was a whirlwind of getting me cleaned up and fed. I was in the hospital for several days because of dehydration and malnutrition. After that, it was off to my first foster family."

I shrug, feeling raw and sensitive. No one at Sea Change knows about my less-than-ideal origin story. They know about the foster families, but being abandoned and left for dead by your mother is too pathetic of a story to burden anyone with.

Keaton pulls me into his lap and wraps himself around me, engulfing me in his strength and warmth. I curl up in his embrace, feeling completely seen and wholly accepted. He doesn't say anything, and he doesn't have to. My man is soaking up all my pain and sadness, leaving me feeling lighter than ever.

"Thank you for sharing that with me," he whispers. "You're so brave, Roxy. So damn strong. I'm in awe of your kind heart, even though life has given you every reason to be bitter. You inspire me."

I lean back a bit so I can look at Keaton. I have no idea how to respond to his sweet words, so I run my fingers through his short beard, loving how he hums in contentment. "Have I earned a glass of wine yet?" I ask, giving him a sassy smile.

"Definitely," he says with a chuckle. He lifts me from his lap and deposits me down next to him as if I weigh nothing.

Keaton pours the wine, and we load the paper plates with food. I take a bite of the sandwich, moaning at the buttery, flaky croissant with prosciutto, some kind of fig jam, and creamy cheese.

Keaton is staring right at me when I open my eyes. "That good, huh?"

"So good," I say with a mouthful of food. Keaton grins and takes a bite, his face twisting in a grimace.

I laugh as he chews and chews and eventually swallows. "You like this?" he asks, his nose scrunched up as he glares at the sandwich.

"Yup! More for me!" I finish the last of my sandwich and grab his.

Keaton laughs, the sound deep and satisfying.

"So," I say after taking a huge bite. "I told you my sob story. Now it's your turn."

Chapter 7

Keaton

Shit.

Roxy is right. I owe her my story, especially after she broke open her heart for me. My chest aches at everything she's been through. I wish I'd met her before now so I could've loved her sooner.

Hold up. *Love?*

Yes, that's what this is. It's official. As I look at my beautiful, strong-as-hell woman, I know it to be true. I feel it all the way through my body, consuming me as I come to terms with this life-altering realization.

"Let's finish this up first, then take a walk along the shoreline," I suggest.

Roxy gives me a knowing look but allows me this extra time before diving into my past.

We talk about our favorite books and movies, some of which we share. I love that we have different tastes. I can't wait to introduce Roxy to new things and to have her show me more of what she loves.

Half an hour later, the food is mostly gone. I know it's time to open up and tell my woman about my past and what brought me here in the first place. Roxy helps me pack everything away, and I set the basket and folded blanket off to the side before holding out my hand for her to take.

Instead of holding my hand, Roxy loops her arm in mine and tucks herself into my side. We take our time walking up the shoreline, and I know I need to break the silence at some point. Roxy doesn't pressure me or push me to talk; she's simply here, supporting me in whatever way I need.

"My old man was a mean drunk with a gambling problem," I finally say.

Roxy squeezes my arm but doesn't say anything, giving me space to get it all out.

"I learned how to take a punch and give one right back at an early age. My father made sure of that. He'd beat me bloody, then tell me to come at him twice as hard."

Roxy gasps softly, then turns her head and presses the lightest kiss to my upper arm. "I'm so sorry you went through that," she whispers.

"It's over now," I tell her as much as myself. It really is over. Truly. He's gone. "My father isn't coming back. He's dead."

I don't think I've said that out loud since getting the news.

"Is that a good thing?" Roxy asks.

"It's..." I pause, not sure how to put my thoughts into words. "Complicated, I guess. I don't talk about this shit to anyone. I haven't seen him since I left home and joined the military right after graduation. That's damn near twenty years ago now."

"When did he pass?"

"Last month," I choke out. Why is my throat clogging up? I can't be getting emotional about this. That's ridiculous.

"Oh," Roxy says softly. "Keaton, I'm so sorry."

"No, it's fine. I'm fine. He was a piece of shit who drank himself to death."

"But still..."

"It shouldn't bother me. It doesn't," I insist, though I no longer believe myself.

"Keaton," Roxy murmurs, coming to a stop at the far side of the beach. "It's okay to grieve what you didn't have with your father. What you'll never have. You don't have to miss him, but that doesn't mean it's not eating you up inside."

I step away from Roxy and run a hand through my short hair, rubbing the back of my neck. I let her words sink in as I stare out across the ocean. The vastness of the sea, the fierce beauty and power behind each wave, calms me, lulling me into a quiet, safe space.

Roxy gently rests her hand on my back, and I can tell she doesn't want to crowd my space. It's thoughtful of her, but I want my woman right here with me. I open my arm, and she clings to my side, wrapping her arms around my torso and resting her head against my chest.

"I didn't know what I was grieving until you said that," I tell her, my voice quiet so as not to break the serenity we've found in our special hideaway. "You're right. The man himself was a monster, but my desire for a father who loved me never left."

"I'm so sorry you went through all that," Roxy soothes. "But we found each other. It may have been a painful journey, but we're here now, right?"

I nod, adjusting our position so we're face to face. I cup the back of her neck and tug her hair so she's looking up at me. My lips meet hers, and I'm surer of it now than ever; I'm completely fucked.

Roxy gasps, which allows me to slip my tongue between her pouty lips and taste her again. She's just as sweet as I remember. I feel her soft hands crawl up my chest, tickling my skin and making me growl into her mouth.

My hands slide down her sides, tracing over the swell of her breasts, the dip in her waist, and the curve of her deliciously wide hips. I grip her there, my fingers digging into her flesh. I almost release my hold on her, not wanting to cause Roxy any pain, but she moans and claws at my chest, letting me know she likes it rough.

Christ, that thought makes my dick ache. I pull her closer to me, needing to feel every inch of her body against mine as I stroke my tongue against hers and swallow down her soft whimpers.

I finally break the kiss, tilting my head up and inhaling sharply. Fucking hell, this woman is addicting. I'll never get enough of her.

Roxy's arms loop around my neck and pull me back down, her lips meeting mine halfway. She owns this kiss. She pulls away, but I follow her, nipping at her bottom lip until she lets me in again.

"Everything aches," she says, her tone somewhere between a moan and a whimper. "I ache for you."

"Fuck," I growl against the sensitive skin of her neck. I breathe in her sea salt and lavender scent, trying to calm the hell down before I maul this precious woman. She deserves better than that for her first time. "Gotta get you inside before we're arrested for indecent exposure," I rasp.

Roxy giggles, making me smile despite the lust raging through my veins.

"Whatever you say," she sasses, letting me take her hand and practically drag her back to my truck.

"That would be a first," I mumble, grinning when I hear Roxy's boisterous laugh.

Ten minutes later, we're back in our motel room. I wish I had thought of renting a better room for the night, like a suite at a fancy hotel with room service and shit.

"This is perfect," Roxy whispers from behind me. I don't know how this woman knows what I'm thinking, but I've stopped asking questions like that. The universe somehow brought me the perfect partner, and I'm not about to waste another second without claiming her.

I turn around, looking into Roxy's ocean-blue eyes, so full of trust. There's an ember glowing beneath the surface, and I know she's as ravenous for me as I am for her.

She gets up on her toes and kisses me, setting my whole world on fire with fresh need for her. My hands find their way under the hem of her dress, gliding up her bare skin. I grip her thick thighs and lift her. Roxy wraps her legs around me, never breaking the kiss. I feel her pussy, hot with need, against my stomach.

"You deserve better," I whisper. "I promise to spoil you once we get out of this situation."

Roxy blushes and nods, though I can tell she's far too in the moment to think about the abstract future. That's just fine with me. I can worry about all of that for us while my woman gets lost in her pleasure.

"Are you ready, beautiful?"

"Yes, please," she pants.

I walk us toward the bed, and her head dips to my neck, licking me and nipping at my skin. Fucking hell, this woman is every dream come true, and I can't believe I get to be her first. Her last, too, if I have anything to say about it.

When we get to the bed, I reluctantly set Roxy down. I find I always want her in my arms, but I realize we have to strip down at some point. I want to see all of her, to feel the heat of her skin pressed against mine.

I'm in a hurry to get my clothes off, now in nothing but my boxer briefs. I notice that Roxy hasn't moved since I set her down.

"Are you okay?" I ask to ensure we're both on the same page.

"Yeah, I just... look at you," she says breathlessly, her eyes roaming over my chest and abs, then lower to my obscene, barely contained erection.

I love that my girl likes what she sees, but I realize she's self-conscious now that I'm nearly naked. "You're the most beautiful woman I've ever seen, Roxy. That first day you walked into the conference room, I felt like all the air was drained from my lungs. You were that stunning. You always are."

I brush my fingertips down her neck and over her shoulder, slipping the strap of her loose-fitting dress off. I repeat the process with the other strap, watching the fabric fall from her body and pile on the floor.

"Jesus, Roxy, you're perfect. Gorgeous. I can't believe you're mine," I tell her honestly.

"Yours?" she asks as I dip my head to her neck, kissing and licking my way down to her collarbone as my hands knead and squeeze her soft flesh.

"Mine," I repeat, licking her ample cleavage and softly biting down on her nipple through the material of her bra.

Roxy moans, and I turn to her other nipple, giving it the same attention. I kneel before her and kiss down her stomach, biting at the waistband of her panties.

"Fuck, you're so beautiful. Love every inch of this sexy body."

I bury my nose into her pussy, breathing in her scent through the lace and reveling in how wet she is already.

"Keaton, please..."

I hear the desperation in her voice and fuck, I feel it too. I look up at my breathtaking woman, a mischievous grin overtaking my features. Roxy opens her mouth, no doubt to ask what's on my mind, but before she can get a word out, I gently push her backward onto the bed. She squeals with laughter, but it quickly turns into a moan as I crawl over her body and cage her in with my arms on either side of her head.

Not able to keep my mouth off of her for another second, I take her lips in mine, savoring her taste and eating up her sexy little sounds. Her fingers grasp my hair, tugging and urging me on. I drag my lips over her jaw, pausing to bite the sensitive skin between her neck and shoulder. Her chest heaves as she pants and moans so sweetly for me.

I kiss my way down her body but have to rest my head on her stomach to catch my breath and get my dick under control. The fucker is ready to explode before we even really get started. Once I've calmed down a bit, I hook my thumbs in her sexy black panties and pull them down her legs. I'd rip them off, but I'm hoping to see her in them again and again.

Placing her legs over my shoulders, I slide my hands under her ass and pull her dripping cunt close to my face. She's glistening with need.

I can see her hard little clit begging me to lick and suck on it. So, I do just that.

"Keaton!" she cries out, and I can tell she's already on edge as her arousal gushes from her tight little hole.

I swipe my tongue up and down her slit before spearing it in her entrance. Roxy bucks her hips and digs her nails into my scalp, pushing me further into her sweet perfection. I love that she's becoming more aware of what she wants. What she needs.

Her pussy twitches around my tongue as I tunnel in and out of her before moving my attention to her bundle of nerves. I bring her right to the edge and then back off. Again and again, I wind her up tight, only to unwind her before she snaps.

I want her to feel this. I want her to reach it. Pure, deep ecstasy.

Roxy whimpers and twists her hips, trying to get the friction she's desperate for, trying to force me to go where she needs me the most. She shakes and tenses with desire, her whole body teetering on the sharp edge of total, mind-numbing bliss. I scrape my teeth along her swollen clit and feel her shatter for me, completely overcome by her pleasure.

Roxy's cries echo throughout the room, sweet music to my ears.

I lap at her release, feeling it drip down my chin. I fucking love it. Fucking need it.

"Keaton, ohmygod, Kea—"

She screams as she comes again, her orgasm slamming into her, leaving her gasping for air. I'm addicted to watching her climax. I need more. Need to feel it with my whole body. Need to give her pleasure with my dick deep inside her.

I gently set her legs down and strip off the last piece of my clothing, revealing my huge, angry cock. Roxy gasps but then spreads her legs for me. I groan at her eagerness, her greedy pussy still pulsing from her orgasms.

I stroke myself a few times as my eyes roam over the most perfect woman I've ever seen. Eventually, I climb back over her and kiss her deeply. She returns my kiss with as much passion as I'm giving her, and then she pulls back and licks her juices off my chin and lips.

"Fuck," I groan as her hot little tongue cleans me up. I settle my hips in between her legs and look into her eyes, searching for any hesitation. "Are you ready for this, beautiful?"

She nods.

"I need your words, Roxy. Be absolutely sure you want this because once I'm inside you, I don't know if I can let you go. Are you ready for that?"

I hold my breath as I wait for her response.

She cups my face and looks into my eyes, filling the emptiness in my heart with so much love and sealing up all the cracks so it can't escape.

"I want that. I want you. All of you. I'm ready."

Never breaking eye contact, I slowly slide my hard length inside her, inch by inch. She's so fucking tight, her walls squeezing around me already. I come up against her barrier and pull back slightly before pushing the rest of the way inside her tight channel.

Roxy's eyes brim with tears, and I hate that I hurt her in any way. She doesn't close her eyes, though. She never looks away, keeping me right here with her. I hold still, giving her time to accept me, to get used to this feeling.

One tear escapes, and I bend to kiss it away.

"I'm sorry, Roxy. You're doing so good. It won't hurt after this, I promise. I'll make you feel so much pleasure. Do you trust me?"

"I do," she whispers. "Kiss me."

I don't hesitate. My mouth finds hers, and I lead us in a slow kiss that quickly turns heated. I feel Roxy wiggle her hips, urging me to move.

"Are you sure, baby?"

"I'm sure. I need... I don't know. I need *something*."

"I've got you, beautiful. I know what you need."

I start with slow, shallow thrusts, and she raises her hips to meet me each time.

"Mmmmore," she breathes as her hips rock faster and faster.

"Fuck," I groan. "You're amazing. You feel so goddamn good, so wet and tight for me."

I pull almost all the way out and slam back inside, causing her to cry out in pleasure.

"Yes! Oh, Keaton, please, please..."

Again and again, I thrust into her, fucking her so deep, hitting the end of her each time. I angle my hips, searching for her most sensitive spot. Roxy's fingernails dig into the skin on my back as a primal sound bubbles up from deep inside her.

"There it is," I grunt, hitting her G-spot harder with each thrust.

"Oh, oh, oh, ffffuck!" she screams. She's so close, so tight, her body stretching and tensing, preparing itself for release.

"Love being inside you. Love fucking you, feeling you, learning everything about your body," I tell her as I pick up speed, jackhammering into her impossibly tight cunt. I'm losing control, and I need her to get there first.

"Come for me, baby. Come on my big cock. Fucking come all over me. I need to feel that pussy pop."

With one final thrust, she cries out, her back bowing off the mattress and then slamming back down as her walls squeeze me so fucking tight. It's the best kind of pain alongside the most intense kind of pleasure.

I lean back and throw her legs over my shoulders, gripping the headboard behind her and pounding into her pussy again and again. I grunt with each thrust, the head of my cock bumping up against her womb, fucking her as deep as possible. Roxy tightens, tenses, twists up in painful pleasure, and then lets go, allowing her orgasm to ravish her curvy little body. Her thighs squeeze my hips as her nails scratch my back. I hope she draws blood. I'll gladly wear her marks.

"Baby... So. Fucking. Good," I snarl, slamming into her one last time, my cock throbbing painfully before exploding inside her.

I roar her name as I pump her full of my cum. Roxy whimpers, milking me for everything I'm worth. Rope after hot, sticky rope shoots inside her, and I swear I see God while I come harder than I ever have before.

I can't breathe, I can't think, my brain and body completely drained of every fucking thing. I collapse and quickly roll onto my back, pulling her limp body across my chest.

We lie there like that for who knows how long while we recover. I stroke Roxy's back and play with her hair, kissing the top of her head every so often. I can't find my voice yet, so I try to do everything I can to show her how much she means to me and how being with her like that was the absolute highlight of my life.

Finally, my heart slows down enough for me to think straight.

"Are you okay, beautiful?"

She nods against my chest but doesn't say anything.

"Look at me, Roxy. Please tell me you're okay. I wasn't gentle." Panic seizes my heart at the thought of hurting her. I lost my damn mind and fucked her like an animal.

Her soft lips place a kiss over my heart before she looks up at me. "I'm good, Keaton. So good. That was..." She trails off.

"Yeah. It was." I reply, unsure how to put what we just shared into words.

I kiss her forehead, cheeks, and nose. Anywhere and everywhere I can reach. I feel her smile, that damn dimple popping out. I kiss it too.

Maybe we don't need the right words. Maybe we just need each other.

I tuck her head back into my chest and hold her, wanting this perfect moment to last forever.

Chapter 8

Roxy

"Morning," a deep voice says, pulling me from the most blissful slumber. My eyes are still closed, but I smile when I feel Keaton's beard tickling my neck before he kisses me there.

"Morning," I whisper, my voice raspy from sleep. Oh, and probably from all the screaming I did last night. My smile grows wicked at the memory, and I know Keaton sees it when he groans.

When I open my eyes, I see my incredibly gorgeous, totally ripped, and completely naked bodyguard leaning over me, his eyes burning with lust.

I lean up, meeting him halfway for a kiss. Keaton breathes me in as he consumes me, each stroke of his tongue winding me up tighter and tighter. When we break apart, Keaton gets off the bed, causing me to furrow my brow in confusion.

"A shower will feel good," he says, confusing me further. "Together," he clarifies.

I take his outstretched hand and let him pull me up off the bed and into his arms.

"Can we both fit in there?" I ask, doubting the size of the shower stall.

"I guess we'll find out."

Before I can say anything else, Keaton dips his head and presses his lips to mine. His kiss is explosive, our tongues warring for control as his hands stroke my body up and down. He cups my ass and lifts me, walking us toward the shower, never breaking the kiss.

Only when Keaton sets me down do we come up for air. He leans over me, turning on the water and ensuring it's warm enough.

"I missed you," he says, turning back to me. "Missed these lips." He kisses me again, short and sweet. "Missed your skin." He kisses across my jaw, down my neck, over my collarbone. "Missed these perfect breasts." He sucks one of my breasts in his mouth while flicking the nipple on my other breast with his thumb. Everything he does drives me crazy with want and need.

"It's only been six hours," I tell him, trying to be sassy. With my breathless tone, however, I'm not sure I quite pull it off.

"Too long," he grunts, leading us into the shower.

The hot water feels good on my sore muscles, but I don't have much time to appreciate that fact. Not with Keaton currently dragging his lips down my body and kneeling in front of me. His hands rest on my hips, guiding me backward so I'm leaning against the shower wall. I guess we fit just fine for his plans.

He nips at my hip bone and blazes a trail of kisses to my other hip bone, where he sucks and nips the skin. I feel his hands massaging my ass, then gripping lower on my thighs.

Keaton guides one leg up over his shoulder, giving him complete access to my soaked pussy. I feel exposed, but not in a bad way. I should be embarrassed, but I'm not. He looks like he's about to go out of his mind with need, and I feel the same.

He turns his head and sinks his teeth into the thigh slung over his shoulder, kissing away the sting.

"Are you wet for me, baby?"

I nod and dig my fingers into his hair, urging him forward.

He chuckles. "You want it bad, don't you, Roxy? Want my tongue inside your juicy pussy?"

Before I can reply, he devours me.

He flattens his tongue and runs it from my entrance to my clit. Again. Again. I buck my hips and moan his name.

"Fucking delicious," he grunts.

Keaton dives back between my legs, spearing his tongue deep inside my channel, causing my pussy walls to pulse around him and release a wave of wetness. Keaton growls, the vibrations echoing off every nerve in my body.

He pulls his tongue out and thrusts it back in, fucking me with his mouth while rubbing my clit with his thumb. It's almost too much. I'm close already. So close...

Keaton withdraws his tongue and finger, and I cry out at the loss.

"I've got you, baby. I'll always take care of you."

He licks my tight ball of nerves, drawing figure eights with his tongue over and over. And then he slams two fingers in my hole, and my body jerks, my back arching off the wall.

Keaton moves his other hand from my hip to my stomach, spreading his fingers out over my belly, keeping me pinned to the wall while also intensifying the pressure I feel building again in my lower abdomen.

"D-don't stop, please..."

He pumps his fingers faster, curling them up and hitting my most sensitive spot. My thighs jerk together, and he strokes the spot again.

"Ah, ah, too much..."

"I've got you. Let go for me. Come all over my face."

He returns his attention to my clit, alternating between fast, slow, hard, and soft licks. Then, he sucks my little nub into his mouth and softly bites down. That's it. My orgasm rips through me.

"Oh fuck, Keaton!" I nearly scream.

He replaces his fingers with his tongue, lapping up all my cum as my pussy convulses around him, squeezing his tongue as he massages my walls. The last of my orgasm fades, and I slump against him. He stands and kisses me, long and deep, slow and passionate. I taste myself on him, and it's so fucking hot. He slides his hands up to my hips, and I throw my arms around his neck, forcing the kiss to go deeper.

He finally breaks the kiss and nuzzles my neck, kissing my shoulder.

"Goddamn, baby. Love watching you come apart in my hands, in my mouth. Fucking beautiful."

He lifts his head and rests it on my forehead. We're both breathing heavily, sharing the same air, the same intensity.

I slide my hands down his neck, over his chest, down his well-defined abs, and grip his hard cock. He hisses and throws his head back.

"Your turn." I grin up at him.

"Shit, Roxy..."

I kneel before him, and he puts his hands on the wall to steady himself. I stroke him a few more times and lick the head of his cock like a lollipop.

"Fuck! Ah..." Keaton clenches his jaw, and I see the muscles in his neck strain.

I feel so powerful, commanding the strength of this beast of a man before me. I open my mouth and slowly ease as much of him into me as I can. He squeezes his eyes shut and throws his head back. I love knowing I am giving him this pleasure. Even though I just came, seeing Keaton like this has me so turned on that I'm ready to go again.

"Goddamn, baby, that's it. That's so fucking it..."

When his length hits the back of my throat, I swallow him down. Keaton's eyes flash open, and a guttural moan rips out of him.

I continue to suck and swallow, massaging his massive length. He looks down at me with awe, and I can't wait to taste him explode in my mouth.

Keaton, however, has other plans.

He pulls out of my mouth with a pop and lifts me into his arms.

"You're incredible, baby girl, but I want to come inside you. Fuck that, I *need* to come inside your perfect pussy."

Before I can respond, he captures my mouth in a frantic kiss, all teeth, tongue, and fire, while guiding me backward until my back hits the wall. He breaks the kiss to lift me into his arms. My legs automatically wrap around his hips, and his hard cock rubs up and down my slit.

"Yes," I moan, grinding against him.

He growls but continues to slide his length through my folds, not penetrating me. His cock slides across my clit, winding that coil deep within tighter and tighter with each stroke.

His mouth roams over my neck, chest, nipples, and everywhere in between. The heat of his tongue and the sting of his teeth peppering my skin set my nerves on fire. My fingers tangle in his hair as I hold on for dear life.

Finally, *finally,* he thrusts his cock deep inside of me while biting down on my nipple. The coil snaps, and I instantly come, pulsing and shaking in his arms. My scream catches in my throat. I forget to breathe. All I can do is drown in wave after wave of pleasure as it washes over me and leaks out from between my thighs.

"Jesus Christ, Roxy, love when you come on my dick. So beautiful, baby. You feel so good." Keaton licks my neck and nibbles at my pulse point. His lips brush the shell of my ear. "Breathe, baby girl. Take a breath for me,"

I drag air into my lungs, the oxygen pulling pleasure along with it while traveling into my bloodstream and coursing through my body.

Keaton chuckles as he pulls my earlobe through his teeth.

"You're so sensitive. I love it. Love seeing you lost in pleasure."

All I can do is moan at this point.

"I have to move, baby."

And with that, he pulls out and slams back into me, setting a punishing pace. Keaton's fingers tighten around my thighs as he holds me in place, pounding into me again and again. It hurts so fucking good, his cock stretching me, his fingers bruising me, his teeth sinking into me.

I tilt my head back, and he covers my mouth with his, swallowing my cries in an all-consuming kiss. He rests his forehead on mine and grunts with each thrust of his hips. I didn't think I had anything left in me, but the pressure builds again in my core, quickly overwhelming me as my legs shake.

What is this man doing to me?

Keaton pulls his head back enough to look me in the eye. His gaze is so intense, but I can't look away.

"One more time, beautiful. I know you can come one more time for me." I close my eyes as I reach the point of no return. "Eyes on me, Roxy. I want to watch it destroy you."

I snap my eyes open right as pleasure overtakes my body. Keaton's cock swells inside of me and explodes as another wave of pleasure vibrates through me, through him, through us, breathing, pulsing together as one.

"*Fuck*, Roxy, Roxy..." he chants my name over and over as the last of our orgasm slips away, dripping down between us.

The moment lasts forever. We never break eye contact, and I can see every emotion Keaton is feeling, just like I know he can see all of me in this moment, so raw and unfiltered.

Keaton sets me down, keeping one hand around my waist while his other hand goes behind me, bracing himself on the wall. We're both still shaking, and it seems Keaton is about as unsteady as I am on my feet right now.

He tucks me into his chest, resting his forehead on the wall, covering me with his entire body like he's shielding me from everything outside this moment. I place a gentle kiss on his chest before burying my head there and wrapping my arms around his waist.

The water quickly grows cold, and we wash up as it turns from lukewarm to ice cold. Keaton dries off, then wraps me in a towel and lifts me into his arms, carrying me the short distance to the bed. We fall onto the mattress, and Keaton adjusts us so he's spooning me.

We must doze off at some point because I'm awoken a bit later by my computer beeping with incoming email. *Crap, I slept in.* When I look over my shoulder at Keaton, I smile to myself. Totally worth it.

I slip out of bed and quietly throw on a maxi dress and a cardigan. Combing my fingers through my slightly damp hair, I make my way over to the couch where my laptop is sitting. I log into my email, my brow furrowing when I see the headline of the email I just received.

Tell no one. Come alone.

Okay, well, that's a red flag right there. Still, I have to know what it says. If this is the person stalking me, this email could contain vital information. It's not like it's out of the realm of possibility that he looked up my work email.

When I click on the message, it's not at all what I was expecting. Instead of threats, it's a lead on one of the major fishing companies on the East Coast. My eyes are glued to the screen as I scroll through the information.

This person has pictures of forged inspection documents and numerous complaints about safety regulations that have been suppressed or ignored over the last decade. They say they have the physical copies of the documents and want to hand them over to someone who can do something about it. Someone who can hold this company accountable for what they've done to the environment and their employees.

In other words, this anonymous tipster is handing me a jackpot of incriminating evidence. I fully plan on using every single document as a reason more regulations need to be put in place and, more importantly, they need to be enforced.

I peer over at Keaton, who is still sound asleep. I grin to myself, pleased that I wore him out so thoroughly. Would he even let me go? Keaton will probably tell me it's too risky, and then I'd miss out on this golden opportunity. Besides, they want to meet on the pier next to Sea Change. It's only a five-minute walk from here, so I could be back before Keaton wakes up.

My stomach twists itself into a knot, knowing somewhere deep down this is a bad idea. But this is my life, dammit! And my career! Yes, Keaton and I have shared some incredible moments, and I very much want him to stick around for a long time, but the truth is, we haven't talked about it. What if he leaves after the bodyguard job is done, and I will have sacrificed the biggest break in my career over nothing?

I don't think he's going to leave. Something in my heart is telling me this is forever. But how can I possibly know that after only a few days? Once again, my head and heart are at war with each other.

My computer beeps with another email, this one in reply to the first.

This offer expires in one hour.

So it's now or never. I choose... *now.*

I type out a response, letting my contact know I'll be there in ten minutes. My chest and stomach feel heavy as I hit send, but I know I made the right choice. I can only count on myself in this life. Keaton might say all the right things and make me crazy with need, but he'll leave. Everyone leaves, eventually.

Gathering my things as silently as possible, I slowly turn the doorknob, not wanting it to make a sound. I carefully open the door enough to slip through, then close it again with just as much care.

I take a deep breath and get my head on straight. This is fine. I'm checking up on a lead. No big deal. I do this all the time. *Then why does it feel so wrong?*

Ignoring the little voice in my head, I make my way down to the pier. The closer I get, the worse I feel. I keep looking over my shoulder, feeling eyes on me with every step. I'm sure I'm just being paranoid.

When I reach my destination, I look around for a man in a navy blue jacket wearing a black New York Mets hat. So far, I've only seen a few dock workers and tourists. I make my way to the right side, where a few shipping crates are stacked. Maybe he'll be here. Less obvious and whatnot.

As I step around to the back of one of the shipping containers, I'm aware of footsteps behind me. I don't have a chance to turn around before an arm clamps around my chest and arms, effectively pinning me in place with a bruising hold. The next thing I know, a cloth is pressed over my mouth and nose. I try to hold my breath, but eventually, I have to inhale.

When I do, my world fades to black.

Chapter 9

Keaton

I wake up with a start, sitting straight up in bed with a sense of panic in my soul. As soon as I look around the room, I know Roxy is gone. Not only do I not see her in this little motel room, but I don't *feel* her. It sounds absurd, and two weeks ago, I would have thought this was all crazy, but it's true. I can't feel Roxy's warmth, her light.

She's gone, and I'm about to bash skulls and scorch the earth to bring her back.

I quickly throw on some pants and a shirt, making a quick pass around the room for signs of forced entry or a struggle. I'm not seeing anything, and I'm sure I would have woken up if anyone came in. Which means Roxy left on her own.

My chest grows tight, and I rub the heel of my hand over my heart to ease the ache. Did she skip out on me? Again? After everything we shared?

No, that can't be right. She surrendered her body to me, gave herself completely to her passion... Not to mention all the past secrets and pain we talked about on our date. I know she felt the connection.

Then why the hell did she leave?

I search for a note or any clue as to where she went. Whatever is going on is fishy. I'd smile at my ocean reference if it weren't for the anxiety and crushing fear that I've somehow lost the only woman I've ever loved.

Fuck, and I didn't even get a chance to tell her that.

In my hurry to get dressed, I didn't notice that Roxy's laptop was open on the coffee table. I shouldn't look, but this is a matter of her safety. It might literally be life or death.

My gut drops at the mention of death, even in my own thoughts. It's not possible. I won't let that happen.

I swipe my finger over the mouse pad, waking up the computer. Thankfully, it's not password protected, though I'll need to talk to my woman about that when I bring her back. She should have more safety precautions on all of her electronics.

But now isn't the time for that lecture. Besides, I have a feeling I'm going to find exactly what I need in here. I figure the only reason my Roxy would leave was for work purposes. As I navigate her email app, I'm thankful she logged in so I don't have to guess her password or wait for someone at Watchdog Protection to hack her account.

The first email that pops up sends chills down my spine, followed by white-hot rage. It's a trap. It's everything Roxy would need to file a lawsuit against a major fishing company and hold them up in court for years. It's a huge win for her and Sea Change. Too bad it's fake. My woman is in danger.

I'll rescue my Roxy and then keep her for good.

I shoot off a text to Logan, asking if he has an update on the analysis of the letter. He's quick to respond, saying he'll call me later this evening. I go ahead and call him, relieved when he picks up.

"She's gone," I say, the urgency in my voice letting my friend know how serious the situation is.

"Shit," Logan mutters. "Here's what I've got so far. The cut out letters all come from the same magazine, which happens to be a publication made for and by employees of the Northeastern Fishing Company, located in Maine. Sound familiar?"

Indeed, it does. "The company Roxy led the protest against. Of course. I mean, I kind of figured, but it's good to have solid evidence."

"We've since narrowed our suspect list to those directly affected by Roxy and Sea Change. Three men with a history of violent crime floated to the top."

I growl over the phone. Logan knows I need those names sooner rather than later.

"Timothy Anderson, Callen Houston, and Ronald Abbot."

I write down the names and ask for a brief physical description of each. Logan asks if I need backup, but I think I can handle it alone. We say our goodbyes, and I promise to let him know if things get out of hand and I need help.

I turn back to the computer, quickly memorizing the location of their meet-up. Grabbing my jacket and keys, I tuck my gun into the waistband of my jeans and head out the door. I don't want to have to use my weapon, but I will if it comes to protecting my woman.

As much as I want to storm onto the pier and tear open every crate while simultaneously throat-punching every person who doesn't help me find my woman, I know that's not a smart plan. I don't know what to expect, so I should do recon first and subtly check the surroundings. Then I can decide what to do from there.

I approach the pier casually, meandering off to one side and sticking to the shadows. There's a flurry of activity here, including unloading giant cargo ships and boat maintenance. It's a noisy place with lots of shadows and areas to hide. Basically, my worst nightmare.

Still, I have to do something. I scan the area for a secluded place, somewhere no one would hear screams or cries for help. My gut twists and I take a calming breath, reminding myself that getting worked up isn't going to help. I need to keep a cool head. Remember my training.

Off to the other side of the pier, I see what appears to be a junkyard for old, abandoned shipping crates. *Bingo.*

Weaving through the rusted-out and decrepit containers the size of semi-trucks, I keep my senses clear and open for any sign of life. It could be movement, an out-of-place noise or, God forbid, the metallic smell of blood.

A tapping sound catches my attention, and I turn my head in that direction. Following the consistent noise, I come upon a crate that appears to be shaking slightly. Everything goes on high alert... until I notice a family of rabbits trying to burrow underneath the damn thing, which is making it rock back and forth.

"Shit," I mutter under my breath, my shoulder sagging in disappointment. Just then, a loud thump sounds from a nearby container, followed by a muffled voice. *Roxy.*

I draw my gun, holding it in front of me as I navigate my way to where I heard Roxy's voice. The closer I get, the less I like what I hear.

"...think there wouldn't be any consequences? You stuffed our boats with lobster shells. How about I cram lobster shells into your mouth, ears, and eyes until you're so mangled your own family won't recognize you?"

Fucking fuck this fucker. What the hell?

A strangled sob fills the air, my heart lurching in my chest at the sound. I can't take it anymore.

I peer around the corner into the open back of the shipping container. My woman is tied to a chair with a gag secured tightly around her mouth. Tears stream down her face, and the look of terror in her eyes is something I'll never forget.

Never again will you feel this way, I vow.

The man in question is Ronald Abbot. He's the only one who fits the physical description Logan gave me. Tall, broad-shouldered, with scraggly blond hair that he usually wears in a rat tail at the base of his neck.

His back is to me, but Roxy sees my face when she looks up. I put my finger to my lips, indicating she can't let on that I'm here. She immediately focuses her attention back on Ronald, though the fear in her eyes has faded somewhat.

Roxy fidgets in her seat and tries to talk through the tight cloth being used as a gag around her mouth. Ronald steps closer to her, and I almost lose my shit. Until I realize she's creating a distraction. Smart girl.

I use the opportunity to silently move forward, stepping up behind Ronald before he knows I'm there. I hook my arm around his neck, choking him as I pull him backward. He raises a hand to fight me off with a dagger, but I block his move, chuckling darkly when his weapon falls to the ground with a clatter.

"What the–"

I kick out the backs of his knees, forcing the fucker to kneel on the hard floor. In a practiced move, I release Ronald from the hold I have on his neck, then press my knee into the center of his back, making him fall forward on his face while I pin him to the ground.

The man tries to scramble away, but I know he's down for the count. Reaching into my back pocket, I pull out a pair of zip ties and get to work, handcuffing his wrists behind his back and tying his ankles together.

"Who the hell are you?" he spits out, turning his head to the side to get a good look at me.

"I'm the wrong fucking man to piss off," I tell him, my tone deadly serious. "I'm the man who is going to ensure you're behind bars for the rest of your miserable life."

"No, I–"

Before he can finish, I stomp kick him in the face. Not hard enough to crack his skull, but enough to shut him the hell up while I call the police.

Rushing over to Roxy, I quickly untie her wrists, gently rubbing the angry red marks I see there. I remove the gag from her mouth and cup her face, streaked with dirt and tears.

"I-I-I'm s-s-sorry," she chokes out.

"Roxy," I say softly, hating that she's crying and broken. "Let's get you home, okay?"

She nods. "Do you th-think you c-could help me p-put my door back on its hinges when you drop me off at my apartment?" My girl is trying to be brave as she stutters through her words, which I respect. I don't like what she's saying, however.

"No, beautiful. I'm not taking you to your apartment. My motel isn't much, but home is wherever you are. Wherever we're together."

Roxy blinks up at me, her tender heart on display. I vow right here and now to protect it until my dying breath.

"You s-s-still want… me?"

I hold out my hand, helping my Roxy stand. Scooping her into my arms, I carry her a safe distance away while we wait for the cops to show up, take our statements, and deal with the degenerate tied up and bleeding on the ground.

Half an hour later, we've been through the interview process with several police officers. I request we return to the station tomorrow to finish any last details. They agree when they see Roxy trembling beneath the blanket they gave her.

"Come on, Roxy," I whisper. "Let's get you cleaned up and in bed."

She nods and slumps into me as if the weight of her existence is too much. I get it. Fuck, do I get it. I pick my girl up, carrying her bridal style to my truck, parked in a shaded, discrete spot.

We're back at the motel within five minutes, and I already have Roxy sitting on the sink counter in the bathroom while I gently wipe off the dirt and grime from her face. Roxy hasn't said much since getting into the truck, but that's okay. I'm just happy she's here with me.

"I shouldn't have gone," she finally says, her voice soft and full of regret.

"You shouldn't have gone *alone*," I correct. "But I understand why you did. If legit, that would have been a huge step forward in your career and saving ocean life."

"I didn't think you'd let me go. I didn't want to disappoint you, but…" She trails off, shrugging her shoulders.

"But?" I prompt as I continue giving my Roxy a sponge bath of sorts while cleaning up the minor cuts and scrapes on her arms. I hate that she went through any of this, but at least she's not hurt any worse.

"But I don't know how much longer you'll be here," she admits softly. "Everyone leaves, eventually."

"Baby," I murmur as I finish cleaning up my girl. "I'm not sure where to start. First, I wouldn't have stopped you from going. I would have insisted that I come along for obvious reasons."

Roxy nods, then hangs her head in shame. Fuck, that's not what I meant, but I have to push forward.

"The ocean is important to you, so it's important to me. Protecting plant and animal life in the sea is your passion, and I want to support you in everything you do. Including taking on large corporations. It's my honor to keep you safe and to watch you grow."

Roxy sniffles, and I catch the first tear on my thumb, wiping it away and then picking up Roxy and carrying her to the couch. When we get settled with her on my lap, I make sure to cup the back of her neck and turn her face toward mine. I need to know she hears me.

"And second," I continue, "I'm not leaving. I'm not abandoning you now my job is technically done."

Roxy stills in my arms, her eyes round with disbelief. It kills me to know she's been doubting us the whole time, but I know it's because of her past and being left behind by her mother. That's okay. I have faith enough for both of us, and I'll show her every damn day that I'll fight for her. For us.

"Really?"

"Really," I confirm. "I'm not sure what the details look like right now, but I'm up for retirement. Remember when I told you my Commanding Officer forced me to take leave?" She nods. "His alternative was permanent retirement. At the time, I couldn't imagine a life without the SEALs. But now..." I lean forward, resting my forehead on Roxy's. "Now, I can't imagine life without waking up next to you every morning. Roxy, I love you."

She lets out a small gasp, and I wait with bated breath for her response.

Chapter 10

Roxy

"You... love me?" I ask, not sure I heard him correctly.

"So much. More than I thought possible," he answers immediately. "Your conviction, strength, talent, and passion are all undeniable," Keaton continues. "And your sassy little mouth might get you in trouble, but it's the kind of trouble I'm growing to love."

I can't help the smile spreading across my lips. He loves me. Keaton loves me.

"I love you, too," I tell him truthfully. "I thought I was the crazy one for falling for you so fast. I was worried I was being clingy."

"Never," he says, wrapping me up in his arms. "Cling away," he encourages, making me giggle. "God, I love that sound. I love you. Everything about you."

I reluctantly untangle myself from Keaton so I can lean back and look him in the eye. "I love you so much," I whisper. "Thank you for caring, for showing me your vulnerable side. Oh, and thanks for the orgasms," I say cheekily because of course I do.

Instead of laughing, Keaton's eyes turn dark and heated. "Can I give you a few more?" His voice is deep and raspy like he's barely hanging on. I suppose life-threatening events and declarations of love are quite the turn-on.

"Are you sore? After beating up that guy?" I ask, not wanting him to hurt himself.

He chuckles. "I'm tougher than you give me credit for. You need a release, Roxy. Let me give it to you."

I look into his golden-brown eyes, seeing nothing but genuine gratitude and love. I relax in his hold and sink into his touch, closing my eyes and letting him take care of me like he wants to. Like I want him to.

"Fine, but just one. I don't want you straining yourself."

"Are you giving me rules now?" he asks in an amused tone.

I shrug, giving him a smirk. "It seems like more your style than mine. Thought I'd try it out."

"Mm-hm," he responds, his voice filled with mischief. "Let's start with a massage."

Keaton rearranges us so my legs and feet are spread over his lap. He digs his fingers into the heel of my foot, working out the knots and rough spots. I moan softly, which elicits a growl from my big, beastly bodyguard.

He moves from one foot to the other and then massages my calves.

"Oh wow," I breathe, sliding down the couch and melting at his touch. "That feels good." I didn't realize how sore my muscles were, but Keaton was right. I needed this massage.

Keaton has a hand on each of my legs, his calloused hands gently stroking my skin and kneading the sore muscles of my calves. Then he trails his tender touches higher up my legs, his fingertips brushing behind my knees and spreading them apart.

The hem of my dress rides up as Keaton bends my knees and spreads them wider. The slight stubble on Keaton's face rubs against my inner thigh, making me gasp and then moan. He presses a sweet kiss there and again on the other side, all the while rubbing soft circles on my thighs with his thumbs.

"Keaton..."

"What do you need, sweet girl?" Keaton murmurs, leaning down to graze his nose and lips against my panties. "Jesus, I can *smell* what you need. Fucking delicious," he growls before sucking on the drenched fabric.

I bow my back and tilt my hips, my reaction completely involuntary. I can't help it. I don't have control of my body anymore. It's Keaton's now.

He grips the waistband of my panties in his teeth, pulling back and then releasing it so it snaps against my skin. I inhale sharply as a shiver breaks out over my entire body. God, he's barely touching me, but I'm already achy and desperate for him. He knows it, too.

Keaton smirks at me from between my spread thighs. Something about that image has me biting back a whimper. He's so damn sexy, especially when he's looking at me like he's running through all the dirty things we're going to do tonight.

I'm about to respond with something that I'm sure is clever and sexy, but when Keaton flattens his tongue and licks my pussy over my lacy panties, all thoughts fly out of my head. He grips the waistband again, this time tugging up so the fabric stretches and digs into my slit, cradling my throbbing clit.

"Ohmygod!" I cry out as the lace scrapes against my sensitive skin. How am I so close to coming already?

Keaton grunts and nips at my soaking folds while pressing his thumb over my clit and rubbing the material into my swollen bundle of nerves. I wiggle and twist beneath him, needing more but not wanting this to end.

I buck my hips and shamelessly rub my pussy against his face. Keaton growls, the vibrations thundering from his chest to his lips and then into my core as I begin to shake and brace myself for the inevitable.

And then he's gone.

"Wh-what?" I gasp for air, my eyes flying open and searching for him. He's standing next to the couch with a cocky grin on his handsome face.

"Let's move this to the bed where you'll be more comfortable," Keaton says smoothly, in direct contrast to my disheveled state.

He holds out a hand to help me up, but I need a minute. My body is still buzzing from my almost orgasm, my pussy throbbing, my lungs burning, my muscles locked and prepared for the release that never came. He peels me off the couch and then leans down, pressing his shoulder into my stomach and standing, effectively tossing me over his shoulder as he walks the few steps over to the bed.

I laugh as he sets me down in front of the bed, wasting no time in getting us undressed. We're a flurry of hands, lips, and sloppy kisses as we pull at each other's clothes. The back of my knees hit the mattress, but Keaton grips my hips, not letting me fall backward. He breaks our kiss and trails his lips down my neck, sucking on my pulse point, my collarbone, lower, lower, until he's licking my nipples.

I arch my back, thrusting my breasts into his face, needing more of whatever he's willing to give me. Keaton grunts in approval, sucking on one breast while kneading the other in his massive hand. I rub up against him, feeling his hot, hard erection graze my center. We both groan at the contact. Keaton grinds into me and sucks my tits, working me over and hurtling my already amped-up body toward an orgasm.

I feel his teeth and tongue everywhere, even though he's only playing with my nipples. Each stroke and teasing bite echoes throughout my body and lands a devastating blow to my clit.

"K-Keaton, it's... I'm..."

He glides his thickness through my folds, holding me by my hips while he continues to worship my breasts. The head of his cock taps my clit just as he bites down on my nipple, and my pussy gushes for him. I hold my breath, waiting for my climax to hit, even though I don't want this to end yet.

The next thing I know, I'm falling backward, my climax and frustration mounting with no means of release.

"Keaton!" I growl in irritation. "I need to come!" I know I sound whiny and desperate. That's because I am. So, so desperate. I'm weak with the need to come. I can't focus on anything else except the ache between my thighs and my trembling muscles.

"Patience, love," he purrs. Keaton is still standing, watching me squirm while fisting his massive cock. He glides his hand up and down in rough strokes. I'm mesmerized by the motion, so much so that I find the strength to sit up and grab hold of him, mimicking what he's doing. "Oh fuck, baby, you feel so good," he groans. I smile, finally feeling like I have the upper hand, so to speak. I lean forward and kiss the tip of his cock, grinning when it twitches. "Christ," he hisses out.

"My turn," I murmur in what I hope is a seductive voice.

It must work because he closes his eyes and tips his head back like he's lost to my touch. I lick the pearl of precum that leaks out of him, moaning at his salty, earthy flavor. Keaton wraps my hair around his fist and draws my head back so I'm looking right at him.

"You want to suck my cock, dirty girl?" he grits out. I nod my head as much as I can and dart my tongue out, flicking it against his throbbing dick. Keaton clenches his jaw, narrowing his eyes at me like he's considering something. Then, he nods once and pushes me back onto the bed, crawling up next to me and settling on his back. "You can wrap those pretty little lips around me, but I need to taste you while you do."

"Oh. Um...how?" I know my face is flushed at my stupid question. I want to do everything with him, but I don't want to disappoint him with my inexperience.

However, one look in his molten eyes puts all doubts and insecurities to rest.

"I forget how fucking innocent you are sometimes. It makes me impossibly hard knowing I get to teach you every goddamn way you can feel pleasure. Now turn around and straddle my face, baby. Ride me while you suck me off."

"Can we even do that?" I whisper, picturing what he's talking about. God, it makes me even wetter. I'd do just about anything this man asked me to.

"We can do whatever the hell we want. And right now, I need to clean up your messy little cunt with my tongue."

I feel my juices drip down my thighs, his filthy words sparking the fire that never went out deep in my core. I scramble to get into position, then hesitate as a wave of vulnerability hits me square in the chest. I feel so much more exposed like this.

Keaton doesn't let me get stuck in my head for long. He grips my hips and pulls me down, sucking on my pussy and making me cry out. He growls and digs his fingers into my flesh while eating me out in sloppy strokes.

I focus on his massive cock once more, licking and kissing down his shaft before opening my mouth and seeing how much of him I can fit inside.

"Holy shit," he barks out, tearing his mouth away from my cunt. "That's it, love, that's so fucking it."

I moan at his approval, taking more of him, sucking him down over and over. I reach out and cup his balls, surprised at how hot and heavy he feels in my hand. Keaton makes a tortured sound in the back of his throat and sucks on my clit, hard, before scraping his teeth against the pulsing little button.

I pop off his dick and drag air into my burning lungs. I rest my forehead on his thigh, trying to catch my breath and steady myself. My entire body is trembling, my muscles tense, my pussy throbbing and soaking Keaton's face as he licks me over and over.

He continues sucking on my clit and circles my entrance with the pad of his thumb before pressing it inside. I slap the mattress with one hand, then ball up my fist, clenching the sheet and twisting it around my fingers.

"Keaton..." I whimper as my hips buck. I can't stop. I need more. Need him to put me out of my misery.

He hums and shakes his head back and forth, nearly making me collapse. I widen my legs and press my convulsing cunt down on his mouth, not even caring how wanton and slutty that makes me. He did this to me. He drove me to the brink of insanity. Now he needs to throw me over the edge and put me out of my sweet misery.

It's right there, so close to the surface I can taste it. My long-awaited orgasm claws at my insides the way I'm clawing at the bed, desperate with the need for release.

"Off," Keaton growls, pushing me to the side.

I land on my back with my legs spread out. Tension wraps itself around my body and pulls every muscle tighter, tighter, tighter, squeezing the air out of my lungs but never letting me find relief.

"No!" I whimper. The need to come is so painful that tears burn the back of my eyes. "Please, please, please..."

Keaton sits up and grabs my hand, guiding it over my quivering pussy lips. He drags my fingers through my soaking slit, making me suck in air when I touch my clit. He grunts and uses my hand to rub furious circles over my swollen bundle of nerves.

I can't concentrate on anything other than the way my body shrinks in on itself, becoming a tight, compact ball of pressure so dense I feel like I might implode and cease to exist. I draw in a huge breath and feel my heart thud against my ribcage once, twice, three times, and then...

Every ounce of tension releases as my body expands and contracts in waves of shuddering bliss. I sob out my orgasm and try to escape from the intensity of it all, but Keaton doesn't let me. He holds my hand down on my clit and continues to rub up and down, side to side, and then in slow circles.

"Again. Make yourself come again, Roxy."

"Wh-what?" I stutter, confused by his words. I can't focus on anything except the scream caught in my throat and the unbelievable pressure building up swiftly in the pit of my stomach. "But... rules..." I say breathlessly, though I'm starting to forget about the rule. I can't think about anything else right now.

I don't understand how it's even possible to be at the peak of one orgasm while another is barreling towards the surface, but when it hits, all the air drains from my lungs as I let out a guttural scream.

"Jesus," Keaton mutters, pressing my fingers against my clit, keeping me right there, forcing my orgasm to reach every empty space, every muscle, every cell before it finally crests and fades.

Keaton helps me turn so my head is next to his and we're on our sides, facing each other. He traces his fingertips over the curve of my hip and the dip in my waist, back and forth, while never breaking eye contact.

I sigh contentedly, then remember I left my man unsatisfied. I had the most incredible climax, but he never came. I was too wrapped up in what he was doing to me to finish him off. Reaching out, I wrap my hand around his rock-hard shaft, making him inhale sharply and dig his fingers into my hip.

"I want to give you what you just gave me," I whisper, gently pushing on his chest with my free hand so he's lying on his back.

"Roxy," he groans. "You give me everything by just existing."

I smile while I climb up his massive, muscled body, straddling him and running my hands up and down his torso. I start with teasing touches, tracing the contours of his abs, pecs, and biceps. His muscles flex everywhere I touch, his skin heating as my pussy pulses. He grunts when I score his flesh with my nails and rock against him, gliding my cunt up and down his thick dick.

"What if I want to give you more? What if I want more from you?" I bite my bottom lip and lift myself on my knees, unsure of what I'm doing but wanting it more than I've ever wanted anything. I hover over his intimidating cock, nestling the tip inside my dripping opening.

"Fuck, take it, dirty girl. Take what you need. Feed that greedy pussy my cock until you come all over me."

My core clenches at his obscene words, making me tremble and suck in a breath. He can be filthy and brutal but also unbelievably sweet and tender. In other words, he's perfect.

Slowly, I ease my way down, every inch of him invading me and filling me up. God, it's too long since we were connected like this. I know he feels it, too, when his hands rest on my hips, holding me in place when I'm finally fully seated on him.

"Love being with you like this, Roxy," he whispers, closing his eyes and breathing deeply.

My pussy tightens around him as if agreeing with his statement.

Keaton flexes his hips, wedging his cock deeper inside me and making us both cry out. I grab his hands from where they are holding my hips and slide them up my body, placing them over my breasts. He takes the hint and squeezes my soft flesh, pinching my nipples.

I wrap my fingers around his wrists and grip him tightly, using his strength as leverage to buck my hips and grind down on him, testing to see what feels good for both of us. I angle my hips, hitting that spot inside me that drives me straight to the edge. I know it feels good for him, too, when he squeezes my breasts roughly and growls.

Lifting slightly, I drop back down on him, hitting that same spot. I bounce on his cock, working us up until we're sweating and shaking. I release his wrists and tangle my fingers in my hair, putting myself on display for my man. He makes me feel seen and loved and so desired. It makes me want to show myself off to him for his pleasure and mine.

"So fucking beautiful, baby girl. So fucking *mine*," he growls, sliding his hands down my back to grip my ass.

He squeezes and separates my cheeks while thrusting his hips, fucking up into me so hard I fall forward. I catch myself on my hands, one on either side of his head.

"Keaton," I moan as he lifts my ass and then shoves me back down on his cock. He's so thick, so long and hard, stretching me painfully, deliciously with each stroke.

My lips meet his in a frantic kiss, teeth clashing, tongues tangling, breaths choppy and uneven as we get lost in our rhythm. I snap my hips against his and bury my face in the side of his neck, unable to hold the weight of my head as a deep, drugging pleasure blankets and burns through me, destroying me in the best way possible.

He slides one hand up my back and fists my hair, pulling my head up and holding it in place while he devours me. Each time he hits the end of me, sparks erupt and singe my nerves. My body feels heavy, swollen, and sensitive, but my head feels like it might float away on a cloud of bliss.

I tear my mouth away from his, gulping down air while he fucks up into me in short, quick bursts. I match his movements as he spears me with his dick, over and over, breaking me apart one thrust at a time.

"Goddamn, look at us. Look at how well your tight little pussy takes my big cock."

I tilt my head down, looking between us. A wave of juices pours out of me, covering his dick, and I whimper, loving the sight of him splitting me open.

"I can't hold on," I whisper, finally looking up at him. Keaton's eyes are black with lust and the need for release. "I-I can't...I can't..."

Something inside me snaps, and I lift my hips and slam my cunt down on him, grinding and swiveling, fucking him desperately, racing toward my end. I can't stop. My body won't let me. My hips refuse to slow down.

I hold myself up with one hand and weave the fingers of my other hand in Keaton's hair, gripping it and forcefully yanking his head up so I can kiss him. His body responds to my manic, all-consuming, obsessive need to fuck hard and fast.

I cling to him as tightly as he's clinging to me, our bodies fusing, grinding, rubbing, causing sweet, white-hot friction to spark a fire that blazes through us both.

"Fuck, fuck, fuck, little girl. Need you to come for me. Need it, need, fuck, please..." he half groans, half growls.

Hearing this mountain of a man beg for me has my heart rattling around in my cage as lava floods my veins. I need to come so badly it scares me. I thought my last orgasm was the peak of pleasure, but the inferno threatening to swallow me whole right now is so much more intense. Flames lap at my nerves, liquid heat coursing through me, filling me up, then leaking out of my convulsing pussy.

"Let go, Roxy. I'm here. I've got you," Keaton reassures me.

I make some undignified sound, then hold my breath, bracing myself for whatever lies on the other side of my release.

Keaton bites my shoulder and hits the very end of me in one brutal thrust. Flames engulf my body, burning me up from the inside out as I come, crying out his name. Tears well up and spill out of my eyes while sweat drips down my skin.

It's too much, yet not enough. I come again, but the ache doesn't go away. Instead, it expands, seizing my lungs and heart, taking control of my limbs as I tremble violently. Keaton holds me close, his hands roaming up and down my back, my ass, my thighs, pressing my body impossibly closer to his like he wants to feel my orgasm with me.

My pleasure spikes again, this time unleashing a tidal wave inside of me. I'm embarrassed by how wet I am, but I can't stop. Every ounce of strength is wrung from my bones as heaving sobs wrack my body.

"Shit, you're squirting all over me. I feel it. *Fuck*, I feel it," he grunts. I have no idea what he's talking about, but I don't have time to dwell on it. Keaton holds me still as he erupts inside of me. I feel his orgasm work its way through his body as he shudders against me. Thick ribbons of cum fill me up and spill out, joining my release as it drips down my thighs and pools on the bed.

I don't know how long we're both suspended in our combined ecstasy, but when I finally come back into my body, I'm curled into Keaton's side, my cheek pressed against his chest, right over his heart. I hear it thundering, his erratic heartbeat matching my own.

"Are you okay?" Keaton murmurs, placing a sweet kiss on the crown of my head.

I nod, a lazy, satiated smile spreading across my lips. "Are you?"

"I'm great." He smirks, cupping the back of my neck and drawing my face toward his. Our lips are an inch apart when he whispers, "I love you so much."

"I love you, too." I barely get the words out before he closes the distance between us.

It's a slow, deep kiss full of gratitude, love, and plans for forever. I instinctively know we'll always kiss like this when we're done making love. This is his promise to me. His commitment. He'll fuck me like we both need him to, but he'll always treasure me.

I sigh contentedly when we break apart, snuggling into his side and resting my head on his shoulder. Keaton rubs my back and nuzzles into the top of my head, breathing me in. The moment is perfect, and my heart is full, knowing we have a lifetime of moments like this.

We still have a few things to figure out, but with Keaton by my side, for the first time in my life, I'm not worried about the future. I know I'll be happy, safe, and complete as long as it includes him.

Epilogue

Keaton

"In closing, I'd like to thank my amazing staff and volunteers for all of their hard work this year. And of course, thank you to our generous donors for another amazing year of saving our oceans. Please enjoy your dinner and drinks!"

Roxy smiles out at the crowd gathered for the annual charity gala for her non-profit, Oceans of Love. She started up her company eight years ago, and so far, they've managed to make major legislation changes when it comes to protecting the sea. Currently, the mission is to lobby congress into tighter restrictions on fishing companies and limit what kind of equipment they can use.

My beautiful, radiant wife makes her way off the stage as everyone in the room claps for her. I'm so goddamn proud of Roxy and how she's grown in the last decade we've been together. While she's always been independent and motivated, I've had the joy of watching her become more stable and confident in herself.

"So, how was I?" Roxy asks as she steps up next to me. I'm always backstage at these events, both as a way to protect her and to support my wife in everything she does.

"Brilliant and gorgeous as always," I tell her, pulling her into my arms.

My wife smiles up at me and gets up on her tiptoes to kiss me. I meet her halfway, always eager for her kiss.

Once we break apart, I turn her so her back is pressed up against my chest. I wrap my arms around her waist and hold my woman as we both look out over the crowd from our spot off to the side of the stage.

"You did all of this," I whisper into the shell of her ear. "You're incredible and you inspire me every single day."

Roxy looks at me over her shoulder, a bright smile on her lovely face. "You're a big part of this, too," she says. "I couldn't have started up my own non-profit and lead protests and political rallies if you weren't by my side. Not only have you supported me in everything I do, but you've been an amazing father to our kids."

I smile and press a kiss to her forehead. She turns back around and leans into me, resting her head on my shoulder while I gently rock us back and forth. Tara, our seven-year-old, has blue eyes just like her mother. She loves swimming, building sandcastles, and making hideous beaded bracelets that we have to pretend to love and wear around the house. I love that girl to pieces.

Maddie, our three-year-old, is already showing us her independent streak, which she no doubt got from her mother. She's always getting into something or storming off on her own. Good thing she has me. I'll protect our little family with every beat of my heart.

THE END

Curious about Warren? Check out his story here![1]

*

Want more deliciously steamy SEAL Team Alpha stories? See the whole series here![2]

*

Interested in Logan & Watchdog Protection, Inc? The entire series is out now![3]

---

1. *https://geni.us/ProtectingLila*

2. *https://sites.google.com/view/sealteamalphaseries/home*

3. *https://books2read.com/u/b5YD0w*

Also by Cameron Hart

Check out my other popular series and books!
Mafia, MC, & Bodyguard Romance:
<u>Moscatelli Crime Family Series</u>[4]
<u>Di Salvo Crime Family Series</u>[5]
<u>Chaos MC series</u>[6]
<u>Savage Ride</u>[7]
Mountain Man Romance:
<u>Men of Blackthorne Mountain Series</u>[8]
<u>Bear's Tooth Mountain Men Series</u>[9]
Cowboy & Small Town Romance:
<u>Roped in by Love Series</u>[10]

---

4. https://books2read.com/u/mqBaze

5. https://books2read.com/u/m0odzW

6. https://books2read.com/u/bMVAOk

7. https://books2read.com/u/bMVlG7

8. https://books2read.com/u/3RYDvB

9. https://books2read.com/u/mVel7A

10. https://books2read.com/u/3RYlBY